The Ghosthunter's Handbook

Herbie Brennan is a professional writer whose work has appeared in more than fifty countries. He began a journalistic career at the age of eighteen and at twenty-four became the youngest newspaper editor in his native Ireland.

By his mid-twenties, he had published his first novel, an historical romance brought out by Doubleday in New York. At age thirty, he made the decision to devote his time to full-length works of fact and fiction for both adults and children. Since then he has published more than ninety books, many of them international best-sellers, for both adults and children.

He lives with his wife in an old rectory in Ireland.

Other books by Herbie Brennan
published by Faber & Faber

Space Quest
111 peculiar questions about the universe and beyond

The Spy's Handbook

The Ghosthunter's Handbook

Herbie Brennan

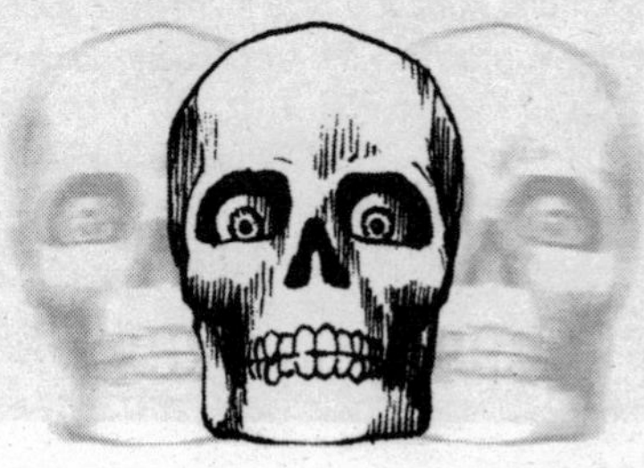

Illustrated by The Maltings Partnership

faber and faber

First published in 2004
by Faber and Faber Limited
3 Queen Square London WC1 3AU

Layout and typesetting by Planet Creative
Printed in England by Bookmarque Ltd

A CIP record for this book
is available from the British Library
ISBN 0–571–21862–8

2 4 6 8 10 9 7 5 3 1

Contents

For Tabs, Toby and Ben with much love from their Uncle

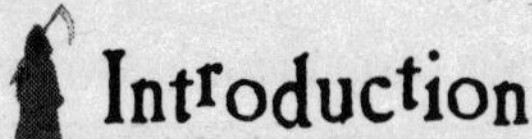

Introduction

Before you start your career as a ghosthunter (professional or amateur) take a little time to consider the following situations.

It's dark. Pitch dark. You're seated with a group of people around a heavy wooden table. The room is so quiet you can hear your colleagues breathing. No-one speaks. No-one moves. You're quite sure of this because you're holding the hands of the people on either side of you and they're doing the same with the people on either side of them...and so on all the way round the table.You feel as if you've been sitting in the dark forever.

A cold breeze blows across the back of your neck as if somebody has opened a window or a door. But still nobody moves.

Then, without warning, a hand touches your face. You jerk back in alarm. "What's the matter?" asks the girl sitting next to you.

Before you can answer, there's a loud cracking sound, like a pistol shot, from the middle of the table. "What was that?" the girl asks in sudden alarm.

"Somebody's acting the fool," comes a new voice.

Another crack, louder this time. Then the table trembles ... shakes... shifts...jerks. Out of the darkness someone moans as the table begins to levitate...

The house stands on a slight rise, a rambling 300-year-old mansion that's seen better days. Silhouetted against the night skyline it looks a little like Norman Bates' home in the old movie *Psycho*...and just as sinister.

You are helping carry a large aluminium case full of sound recording gear. Some way ahead, two of your companions are struggling with a similar case packed with video equipment.

The house is deserted and locked, but you have a key. The man holding the other handle of your case has written permission from the owner to enter. The owner is in Australia. Nobody lives in the house any more. Nobody has lived here for more than fifteen years.

Inside, the house smells of damp. Furniture and carpets are long gone so your footsteps echo eerily on the floorboards. Everyone in your group begins to whisper as if they'd just entered a cathedral.

You're an experienced team and each of you knows exactly what to do. Working to a pre-arranged plan you begin to set up the recording equipment – in the cellar, in the empty bedrooms upstairs. Then you select a ground-floor room to act as your headquarters and install the monitoring equipment there.

There's no electricity in the house, so everything has to be connected to a portable generator. As it starts up, the lights come on and you heave a sigh of relief. No more poking about with flashlights and battery-operated lamps.

One of your engineers throws the switches on the monitoring equipment, checking each item as he goes. One by one the screens flare into life. Selected members of your party, stationed round the house, call out a tight little speech from Shakespeare to test that the audio equipment is functioning properly.

As you glance towards the monitors, something catches your eye. The camera set up in the cellar pans slowly in an ever-repeating arc that brings most of the room into view. Towards the end of the arc it dips slightly and you catch a glimpse of the floor.

Someone has drawn a large circle there in paint or chalk – it's difficult to be sure which. Weird symbols have been drawn all around it. The last time you saw anything like this was in a horror movie about black magic.

All the members of your group now withdraw from the rest of the house to congregate in the headquarters room. The door is firmly closed. Everyone sits back to wait.

At first all eyes are glued to the monitor screens, but as midnight comes and goes, eyes grow tired and attention wanders. You find yourself dozing off…

At eight minutes past two in the morning you are jerked awake by a sudden howling scream. "What's the matter?" you demand of your companions.

But none of them has screamed. The sound, still broadcasting from the loudspeakers, is coming from the empty cellar…

You are attending a séance in Wales. The medium claims to be able to materialise spirits of the dead – not just make them visible, but make them solid as well. You don't believe a word of it, of course. You've read dozens of Sunday newspaper stories about fake mediums.

The séance is held in a small, overheated room at the back of a red-brick semi-detached council house. There's a large curtained cabinet to one side which the medium says is where the spirits will manifest. You and others of the group take your seats in uncomfortable wooden chairs arranged in a semi-circle around the cabinet. The medium turns out the main lights and takes his own seat in the centre.

The room is now illuminated by a small, red lamp of the type used by professional photographers in their darkrooms. At first you can see nothing at all, but as your eyes adjust, more and more details of the room become visible. Soon you can see almost as easily as in daylight.

The medium asks everyone to say a short prayer, then cautions absolute quiet. He warns that whatever happens, everyone should keep their seats and avoid panic.

Your group sits quietly and waits. After a few minutes, the

medium begins to breathe strangely and his head slumps down on his chest. Somebody whispers that he has gone into trance. Suddenly, in a deep sepulchral voice he asks, "Is anybody there?"

It's as much as you can do not to giggle. This is so corny it's amazing anybody could be taken in. It's no surprise to you when the curtain on the cabinet begins to shake. Behind you somebody coughs. Somebody else whispers, "Look!"

You're looking all right – looking at the phoniest circus act you've ever seen. The shaking curtain is now drawn back and out of the cabinet steps the first 'spirit manifestation.'

It's the figure of a man, around average height but decidedly overweight. His face is pale as a corpse, but it's a floury pallor, as if somebody had dusted him with make-up. He is wearing a shiny, ill-cut Sunday suit and, incredibly, hobnail boots. "Ah," murmurs the medium, his head still on his chest, "we are honoured by the presence of the great Sir Arthur, who has returned to us to give the sceptics amongst you proof of the Afterlife."

This has to be a gag. The Great Sir Arthur walks twice around the room, his hobnails clumping on the floor. There is an excited murmur among those present, although how anyone can take this sort of performance seriously is completely beyond your understanding.

To your surprise, the Great Sir Arthur stops in front of you and sticks out his hand. "Do not be afraid," the medium intones. Afraid? The only thing you're afraid of is bursting out laughing. "Pleased to meet you, Artie," you say cheerfully as you reach out to shake his hand.

It feels cool, but firm. Sir Arthur smiles at you then, while still holding your hand, gradually disappears…

There's a pop concert you don't want to miss on the radio, but you're going to a party that night so you dig out a C90, plug in your cassette recorder and set the timer to record it.

The party's a blast. You get home far later than you promised and have to creep in through the back to avoid waking your folks and sending your old man ballistic. You hit the sack and crash at once, sleeping like the dead.

Next day is Saturday – no school! – so your old lady lets you sleep through. You surface sometime around eleven, crawl downstairs and help yourself to cornflakes. Your old lady comes in and nags until you agree to mow the lawn. Your old man comes in and nags until you agree to help him clear out the shed. There goes Saturday. It's after teatime before you remember about the pop concert and go up to your room to check the recording.

You rewind the cassette, then hit the play button. There's a station ident and the DJ says cheerfully, "Hey, a big treat now for all you –" And that's it. Nothing more from the speaker except a static hiss.

What's happened here? Maybe there was a technical fault at the station. Maybe your cassette recorder wasn't set right. Maybe the tape was duff. Whatever the reason, it looks like you've lost your pop concert.

You fast forward a bit in case you've caught some of it, but there's still nothing except that static hiss. You leave the tape running as you search in your cupboard for a clean shirt and jeans.

There was something on the tape! Sounded like a woman's voice, calling your name. You stop and listen. Nothing. You go back to the recorder and rewind, then play, listening intently. There it is again! Faint, but quite distinct – a woman's voice calling your name.

You rewind, hit the volume, then play back again. No doubt

about it – the voice is definitely there, calling you, calling you. What's more, you recognise it at this volume. It's the voice of your Nan, your grandmother. You'd know it anywhere.

Except your Nan died eighteen months ago…

What did you think of those stories?

First of all, did you believe them or not? Did you think they were a load of rubbish, lies from start to finish, stupid little fictions? Did you think some might be true, but others were just too weird? Or did you suspect you were reading the truth, the whole truth and nothing but the truth?

Then after that, how did they make you feel? Were you a little jittery while you were reading them? Did the punch-lines make you nervous, maybe even shocked or frightened? Did you give thanks that stuff like that only happens to other people, not to you?

You have my word that every story you've just read is based on fact. Nothing of importance has been added, nothing exaggerated. Let me run through them again briefly:

The first story was based on a table-turning experiment carried out in England, within sight of the Malvern Hills in the Midlands, a few years ago. I was there. The movement of the table eventually became so violent that it bounced across the room and trapped me against a wall.

The second story was based on the investigation of a haunted house called Gill Hall. It's burned down now, but it once stood lonely and abandoned outside Dromore in County Down, Northern Ireland. It was investigated by a team of psychical researchers using the most up-to-date electronic equipment money could buy. I listened to the tapes. The sounds picked up in that empty house were extraordinary – whispered voices, crashes, screams… Even the business about the circle drawn on the cellar floor was true. Somebody had broken in and used the place for an unpleasant black magic ritual.

The third story was based on the experience of an old friend of mine – Desmond Leslie, now dead, alas – at a séance in Cardiff. When the 'spirits' began to crash about, he was utterly convinced the whole thing was a fake. So much so that he gripped one by the hand and held on firmly, hoping to expose the fraud. But the entity dissolved before his eyes.

The fourth and final story was based on something that happened to a Swedish film producer and amateur ornithologist named Frederick Jurgenson. He was recording birdsong in some woods near Stockholm when he discovered the voice of his dead mother calling him on the tape.

If that sort of thing makes you nervous, maybe you should put away this handbook. Because you've only read a fraction of the spooky material that awaits you in the pages still to come.

But if you can't wait to meet your first ghost, then this is definitely the book for you. In it you'll learn how to tell fake ghosts from real, how phoney ghosts are manufactured and how real ghosts manifest. You'll learn about the different types of ghost and where to look for them. You'll discover what equipment you'll need and how to make it. In short, you'll have everything you need to embark on a fascinating new experience.

Welcome to the weird and wonderful world of ghosthunting.

1

The Ghost Box

Before you do anything, you should make a Ghost Box. That's to say, you should put together your ghosthunter's kit, a collection of equipment – including this handbook – that will help you track or contact ghosts. You won't literally need a box, although you can use one if you like – a briefcase or rucksack would be better since that will allow you to carry a range of equipment with you when you go hunting.

In this section I'll concentrate on how to put your Ghost Box together, rather than how to use the equipment included. This may be a bit frustrating if you're anxious to get started, but worry not – you'll find full instructions on how to use every item later in this handbook. Let me start by telling you what to do with your coathangers…

Ghost Rods

To make this piece of equipment, you'll need two wire coathangers. These are the hangers they use to send back your dry cleaning. Have a look in your mother's wardrobe: there are probably so many in there that she will never miss a couple.

Next, equip yourself with a pair of wire-cutters. Look in the family toolbox. If there are no proper wire-cutters, check out the pliers (every toolbox has them) which will almost certainly have a wire-cutting blade just beneath the grips.

Take a good look at one of those coathangers. You'll find it's made from a single stiff piece of wire, twisted into shape. The join is usually at the top, underneath the hook. Now follow this simple four-step plan:

Step 1
Start with your basic wire coathanger.

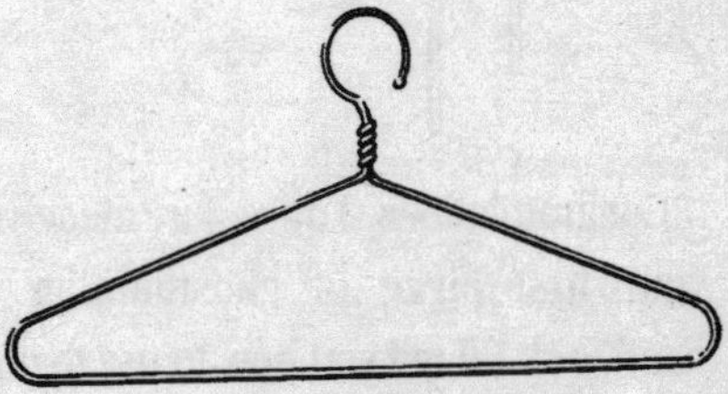

Step 2
Untwist, so it begins to open.

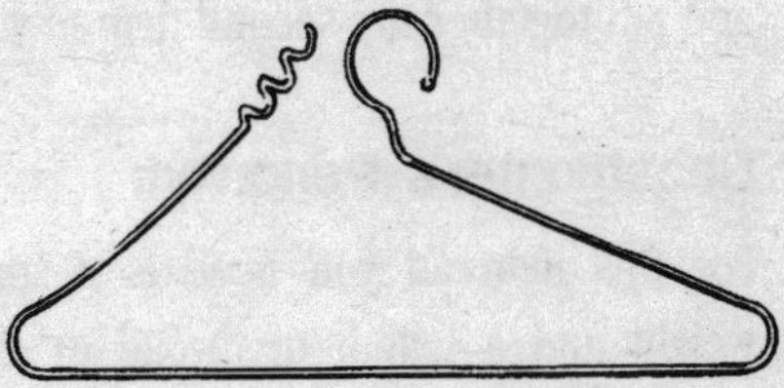

Step 3
Bend into a rough L-shape.

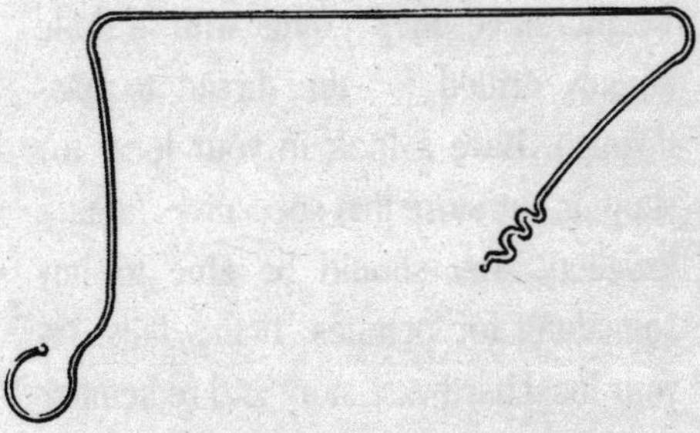

Step 4
Use wire-cutters to trim the ends.

Ideally, the short leg of this L shape should be a little longer than the width of your hand. Now repeat the entire process with the second coathanger so you end up with two identical L-shaped rods, like this:

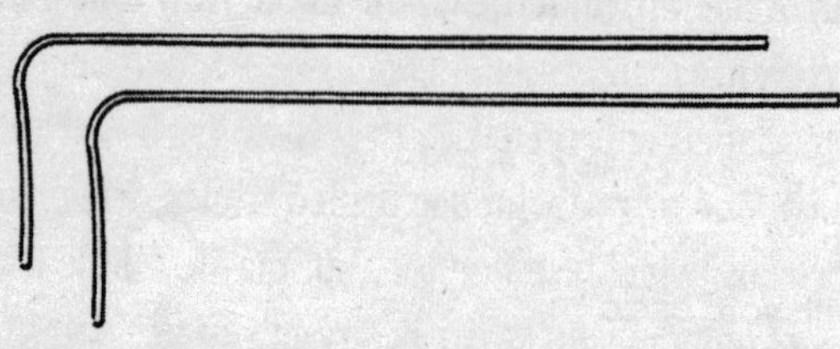

Congratulations. You've just made yourself a set of Ghost Rods, your first piece of ghosthunting equipment. Later in this handbook I'll tell you how to use them. But for now, let's press on and put together the second item in your Ghost Box.

Ghosthunter's Pendulum

For this item all you need is a small weight and a length of thread or thin cord. Metal beads work well for the weight since they come with a hole already drilled for the thread to pass through. Have a look in your local toy shop or any store that specialises in junk jewellery. You should be able to buy something for pennies. If this fails, try your local hardware store and remember you can improvise – it doesn't have to be a metal bead. You might even be lucky enough to find a small weight like the one illustrated, with a loop you can use to attach the thread.

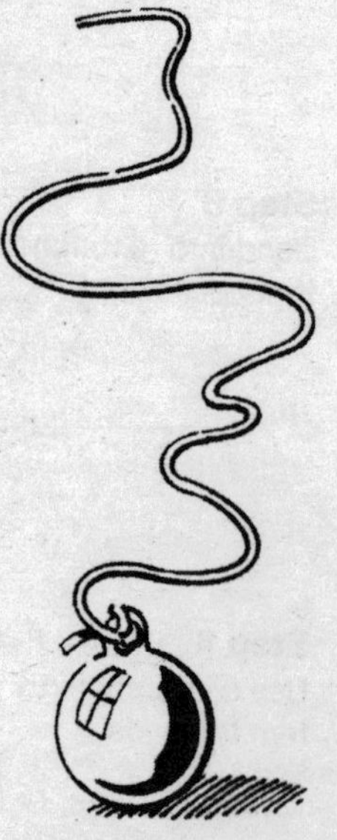

The chances are you'll sometimes have to use your pendulum outside, possibly in windy conditions, so you should avoid picking too light a weight. But don't buy anything really heavy either. Something around 14 grams is about right.

If you prefer to use wood for your weight, that's good too. I know quite a few ghosthunters who use wooden pendulums and, properly shaped and polished, they look great and work well. I even know one or two who use drilled stones, which are fine, or small crystals, which are fine too, but maybe a little tricky. You'll find lots of hunters who swear by crystals in this sort of work and while I agree crystals can give you excellent results, I wouldn't recommend them for beginners. If crystals interest you, take time to study their properties before you start thinking of one for a pendulum[1].

Apart from that, the only other real concern about the weight you use is to avoid synthetics like nylon or plastic. They'll still work (usually) but they won't work half as well as metal, wood, stone, crystal or even glass.

For your thread, try to avoid using anything with a twist. This more or less rules out anything you'll find in the average sewing box, since commercial thread is manufactured by twining fine strands around each other. But this is no loss since commercial thread will snap too easily to make a good pendulum. Look for thin cord without a twist, or nylon thread. A single filament piece of fishing line is ideal and certainly strong enough for your needs. Cut about 1 metre and attach it to your weight.

That's it – you've made your ghosthunter's pendulum! Like the rods, I'll tell you how to use it later.

[1] I'd recommend *Crystals For Life* by Jacquie Burgess. (Published by Gill and Macmillan.) I believe this is the best reference book on crystals in the history of the universe, a belief wholly uninfluenced by the fact that I am married to the author.

Ghost Report Forms

One of the things you're going to find as a ghosthunter is that lots of people don't believe in ghosts. There's a reason for this. Actually there are several reasons, but one of the most important is that far too many ghosthunters are sloppy in their work. They don't take notes, they won't keep records. As a result, many highly evidential cases of genuine hauntings never see the light of day.

You won't be like that, of course. And just to make it easy for you, I've included a special Ghost Report Form at the back of this handbook. It'll make it really easy for you to keep records of all your spooky experiences.

Since the best time to write up your record is immediately after you've seen the ghost, make up a batch of, say, 25 photocopies of the form and keep them in your Ghost Box.

There are several additional items you'll need for your Ghost Box, but these you'll have to buy if you don't already have them.

Notebook and Pen

These are the cheapest of the items you'll have to buy… and the most important. Your Ghost Report Forms are all very necessary, but you'll generally fill those out after the event. You'll need a notebook and pen to keep track of what's going on, including what you're experiencing inside, during the event. Pick a notebook that fits easily into your pocket and has a hard back so you can use it anywhere. A ball-point is probably the best pen to use. Invest in a good one and keep a spare.

Cassette Recorder

It's perfectly possible to capture psychical phenomena on tape – I've listened to the evidence often enough. The gear used in the

Gill Hall ghost hunt was expensive reel-to-reel machinery with super-sensitive professional quality microphones, but these days cassette decks have become so sophisticated and sensitive that they'll take you a long way. They're also a lot easier to carry and you can use them to take notes and interview witnesses as well as recording phenomena directly. Use a separate microphone if at all possible – there are drawbacks with the built-in variety which usually make them less sensitive. Equip yourself with a good supply of the longest-play cassettes your machine will handle: C90s for most decks. The new digital recorders seem to be getting good results, but relax if you don't have one: they're no better than the tape machines.

Camera

What's the best camera to use for hunting ghosts? That's like asking how long is a piece of string. The plain fact is some excellent photographs of paranormal phenomena have been taken using simple, inexpensive snapshot equipment. Here are a few of your options:

Disposable camera. Available from most large chemist's. They're cheap and cheerful. You point, click, use up your film then get it processed and throw the camera away. Most come with a built-in flash. Most give surprisingly good results so long as you're not looking for artistic photography, which you won't be when you're ghosthunting.

Polaroid instant camera. There are pros and cons here. The cons are that most instant cameras of this type produce fairly small pictures and getting enlargements is a bit difficult. The pros are that you can see within a minute whether you've got a

picture of a ghost and you'll get far less flack about faking it if you have. Polaroid pictures aren't impossible to fake, but it's far more difficult than tweaking a standard print.

Snapshot camera. Not at all a bad choice. Some interesting results have been obtained with just this sort of equipment. If there's a drawback, it's that snapshot cameras don't always cope well with low lighting conditions and there are lots of times in a ghosthunter's career when you won't be able to use flash.

Expensive interchangeable-lens big-deal professional camera. Just about as good as you'll get, but the problem will always be the first word of the description – this sort of gear can be very expensive. If you've money to burn, however, this is the type of camera you should be using. Bring a tripod, stop down the lens and you could be surprised what you'll pick up in the right environment.

Digital camera. Let me come right out in the open and admit I don't know for sure about this type of camera. At time of writing, digital cameras are too new on the market to have shown their particular strengths and weaknesses in psychical research. Also at this time they're expensive as well, although the prices generally are coming down. That said, from what I've seen of digital cameras, they should give good results in ghosthunting and if Granny has just given you one for your birthday, you'd be well advised to experiment.

That's just about everything you really *need* for your Ghost Box. With the equipment listed, you could ghosthunt comfortably – and scientifically – for the next 10 years. But there are a couple of additional items that will allow you to expand your activities quite dramatically. They're not necessities but, if you can afford it, it would be useful to add a video camera to your kit; and if you can find it, add a diode (a small gizmo you can buy from specialist amateur radio-builders' shops) as well. You'll find out why later in this handbook.

2

Spotting Fake Stories

Once they find out you're a psychical researcher, every joker in the country will swoop down with his own ghost story. They think it's so fun to make up something silly then see if they can sell it to the poor gullible ghosthunter. Trouble is, many jokers' stories sound convincing. If you want to avoid wasting your time on wild goose chases, you need to know how to spot the fakes.

Here are a few ghost stories drawn from the archives of psychical research and my personal files. I'll give you a little background to each, but the important thing is you're getting the story as told. Your job is to decide on a case-by-case basis whether the particular story is true or false. Remember, you're not trying to decide whether the ghosts were really ghosts. You're trying to decide whether the person concerned really did have a peculiar experience (whatever the explanation for it might be) or whether he or she was making up the whole story.

The only bit of advance advice I'm going to give you is to tackle the job with an open mind. All of the stories may be fake, all of them may be true, or you may be looking at a mixture – some fake, some true. Make each decision as you go along. Use logic and common sense, perhaps mixed with a little intuition. Afterwards you'll find out how well – or badly – you did.

Story One

This story was told by a well-known rally driver, who later went into the garage business. Although at first he only mentioned it to a few close friends, the story was eventually published.

It was midnight on Hallowe'en. Two close friends tramped across open fields to an ancient ring-fort set in a remote location on a private country estate. One was a tenant of the estate, the other a visitor from another country.

Together they entered the ring-fort, which was comprised of a 7-metre high earthen rampart surrounding a single megalithic standing-stone placed at the exact centre. Beneath the standing-stone was a Bronze Age cyst grave (a narrow, slit-like burial place) that had been investigated by archaeologists several years before and found to contain the bones of a woman and a wolfhound.

Neither of the friends carried an electric torch or any other form of light, but while it had been raining heavily earlier, the clouds were now breaking up and there was intermittent moonlight.

They walked over to lean on the low metal fence the archaeologists had left to protect the standing stone. After a moment, one of them was struck by an eerie sensation and grew frightened. "Let's get out of here!" he said.

They both turned and began to walk quickly from the ring-fort. As they did so, a herd of some 25 tiny horses, each ghostly white and no larger than a cocker spaniel, appeared out of nowhere at the top of the earthwork and galloped along for several yards before disappearing.

2

The friends looked at one another, then ran. When they reached the field beyond the earthwork there was no sign of the phantom horses. Nor was there any sign of livestock such as sheep, which they might have misidentified. Later, one of the pair discovered that ancient megalithic sites are traditionally associated with the appearance of fairy horses.

That's the story. Read through it again and examine the specific details. Midnight at Hallowe'en sounds terribly corny. And how about that grave? Would archaeologists still find bones at a site dating back as far as the Bronze Age? Come to that, is anybody likely to venture out into the fields at night without a torch, even if there was an occasional glimpse of the moon? Most important of all, do you buy that incredible story of tiny horses? Decide now, tick the relevant box below, then go on to the next story.

False ☐ True ☐

Story Two

This story was originally told by a weekly newspaper editor who went on to investigate the background of his experience, but did not then or later publish a story about it in his paper. The account here is given in his own words.

I was working late in my first-floor office one evening when I heard footsteps coming up the stairs. I assumed it was our newspaper photographer en route to his darkroom, which was on the same floor. But while my office door was wide open nobody passed it.

After a few moments, I went out to investigate. The darkroom was empty, as were the remaining offices on the first floor. I went downstairs to the newspaper's reception area, but that was empty as well and the front door securely locked.

Thoroughly bewildered by now, I went back upstairs, but continued up to the second floor, which consisted of a single undivided room used to store old newspapers. No-one was there.

There was only one entrance and exit to the office building and only one set of stairs to the upper two floors. Six people were keyholders to the building, including myself. The following day I asked the other five if they had called to the office the previous evening, but none had. There was no sign of any robbery or break-in. Nonetheless, I was quite certain of what I had heard.

Although the footsteps were loud, distinct, 'solid' and not at all ghostly, I began to wonder if I had had a paranormal experience. When I investigated the history of the office building, I discovered that many years before, when it was still a private house, a tenant had climbed the stairs and hanged himself on the landing.

Well, that's a classic ghost story – somebody commits suicide and his ghost walks the stairs forever more. But do you believe it? You might like to ask yourself why the editor never published: the whole thing sounds like an excellent story for a weekly newspaper. Would you really

have an office building with only one entrance and exit – isn't that against fire regulations? And isn't it a little suspicious that he never knew the building's history before he investigated? Make your decision below, then go on to the next story.

False ☐ True ☐

Story Three

Since this story has appeared in the published autobiography of the man involved, I feel free to mention his name. These are the facts of a very peculiar experience reported by Alfred Sutro, a wealthy, well-known and distinguished British playwright in the 1930s. It was, he said, the only time in his life he ever encountered anything of a psychical nature.

Alfred Sutro was being driven along a country road when he heard what he thought might be a child crying and asked his chauffeur to stop. The car pulled in and Sutro asked the driver if he could hear anything. The chauffeur listened, then shook his head. He could hear nothing.

But Sutro could. In fact he could hear a child crying so clearly now that he was able to follow the sound behind some trees and down a slope to the bank of a river. There he found a pretty little girl of three or four, sobbing bitterly and soaking wet. Sutro realized she must have fallen into the river. He gathered her up and carried her back to the car, but could not get her to stop crying long enough to tell him what had happened.

When he asked where she lived she would not tell him, but then Sutro pointed ahead and she nodded. He instructed the chauffeur to drive on. A short distance away they came to a gate.

The child became excited and pointed towards it. Sutro instructed his chauffeur to drive in.

They travelled up the driveway to the front door of a largish house. As Sutro got out of the car and headed for the door, a man and woman rushed out, both very obviously upset. "Have you any news of the child?" the woman asked.

"She's in my car," Sutro told her, greatly relieved. But when they went back to the car, it was empty except for the driver.

"Where's the little girl?" Sutro asked.

The man looked at him blankly. "What little girl?"

"The child I brought in the car," Sutro said.

"You didn't bring any child in the car," his chauffeur told him.

Accompanied by the parents of the missing child, they drove back to the river bank. There was the body of the little girl, drowned in a few metres of water. Sutro had carried back her ghost.

Wow, that's one for the archives! If it's actually true, that is. You need to ask yourself how come Sutro missed seeing the body the first time he went down to the river bank. And if the parents had already discovered the youngster missing – as they clearly had – why wasn't the whole area swarming with police? So true or fake? The decision is yours.

True ☐

2

Story Four

A successful advertising executive was the source for this one. He was known for his interest in peculiar phenomena, but claimed never before to have experienced anything supernatural himself.

It was a dry, warm, sunny summer's weekday morning. The executive concerned was sunbathing in a 17th century walled garden near his home when a young woman appeared.

She was about 28 years old, dark-haired and pretty. Curiously, she was wearing period costume, an ankle-length beige crinoline, full at the bottom. The executive assumed she must be trying out a costume for a fancy dress party.

She walked across the lawn, passing no more than a few metres in front of the executive, but made no answer when he called out "Good morning." He watched her cross the lawn towards a rose bower. When she reached the low box hedge she shimmered briefly, then disappeared.

The man jumped up and ran the few metres to the hedge. There was no sign of the young woman. The hedge itself was less than a metre high, too low to give any cover. Besides, he had been watching when she vanished. The conclusion was obvious. The girl was a ghost.

Or was he lying in his teeth? You have to ask yourself what a successful executive was doing sunbathing when he should have been at work. And how did he gain access to what was clearly a private walled garden? Check the account for any other questionable elements, then make your decision.

False ☐ True ☐

Story Five

This one appeared in the parish magazine of a small village in Northumberland. The original account was unsigned, but investigation by a psychical researcher subsequently revealed the author was the local vicar who claimed he had verified the events to his own satisfaction.

The village doctor kept a talking parrot in his waiting room to entertain his patients. During a weekday afternoon surgery in May, 2001, the bird suddenly began to call out "Help me!" in a perfect imitation of the voice of a local grocer.

Coincidentally, among the patients in the waiting room was the grocer's wife who grew nervous when the bird persisted in its eerie call and eventually left the surgery to return to the shop. There she found her husband lying dead on the floor just inside the door. The doctor later confirmed he had suffered a fatal heart attack just minutes before the bird began to speak with his voice.

The parrot had never imitated the grocer's voice before, nor did it ever do so again after the day of his death.

There have been well-attested cases that seem to point to possession, but doesn't possession of a parrot sound a bit far-fetched? And don't you have to ask yourself how the grocer could have had a massive heart attack in his shop without any of his customers noticing? As always, it's your choice –

False ☐ True ☐

Have you checked the boxes after each story? Don't read on until you do because this is the point where I'm going to spill the beans about which, if any, of the stories is true and which, if any, is faked. You may be in for a few surprises. Here's the truth about each story:

Story One

Midnight at Hallowe'en sounds too good to be true for a ghost story, but the fact remains that ghosts can appear any time they please. Bone remnants will easily survive from the Bronze Age, so there's no discrepancy here. Would two sane and sensible individuals venture in the fields at night without equipping themselves with electric torches? Apparently they would. This story is true.

Story Two

This one's true as well. The editor never even considered publishing it in his newspaper because he hated personal publicity. There was no reason why he should have investigated the history of his office building before he began to suspect it might be haunted.

Story Three

Although published as fact in Alfred Sutro's 1933 autobiography

Celebrities and Simple Souls, this story is a fake. Sutro subsequently admitted it and said he dreamed the story up to show how easy it was to fool people who believed in ghosts … and to find out how many people would hit on the most obvious solution to the mystery of the ghostly child – that he was lying. (Apparently nobody did. The story stood as a fascinating example of a paranormal experience until he issued his confession.)

But even without the admission, it should have been possible for you to figure out his story was phoney because there were incidental details that didn't ring true. This is where you get to the real secret of spotting a fake story. Don't get mesmerised by the psychical phenomena, which are likely to sound unbelievable by their very nature. Concentrate instead on incidental details. If the details hold up, then the story may be worth investigation. If not, you can safely dismiss it as fake.

What are the telling details in Sutro's story? Well, let's start with the claim that he was sitting in his car when he heard the sound of a child crying. Next time you're in a car, try listening very carefully, then ask yourself how many conversations you have overheard from people walking on the pavement. Even with the roof down on a summer's day, the answer is precisely none while the car was moving.

Sutro didn't have the roof down, didn't even claim to have a window open. So he had no chance of hearing a child crying at the side of the road, let alone down a bank and behind some trees.

You might argue that whatever he believed, Sutro didn't actually hear the sound, merely picked up a psychic impression. But then you have to ask why he didn't find this strange? He stated very clearly he was no psychic and spoke of the crying as if it was the most ordinary thing in the world. But it wasn't. It was an impossible sound.

2

As you continue to examine Sutro's story, additional weaknesses emerge. For example, he claims that when he found the little girl, he picked her up and carried her back to the car. But later, his chauffeur was supposed to have said there was no child in the car at any time.

Both these statements can't be true. If there was never anyone else in the car, then Sutro must have looked very odd carrying an invisible child. Why didn't his chauffeur ask what on earth he was doing… or at least comment on his strange behaviour? If, on the other hand, Sutro really did carry a child into the car – possibly as some sort of temporary manifestation – why did the driver claim he never saw her?

Imagine yourself at the scene. Sutro claimed he was trying to persuade the girl to stop crying and tell him where she lived. If no child was there, wouldn't you wonder who he was talking to? Of course you would… and so would the driver. Yet the chauffeur clearly noticed nothing amiss until he was questioned about the missing child.

The inconsistencies continue in the part of the story dealing with their arrival at the house. Sutro claimed he got out of the car and was met by the parents. But he got out of the car, leaving the child behind.

Ask yourself how likely that was? Bear in mind he was supposed to believe the child was a living, breathing, dripping youngster. Surely, if he thought he'd found her home, he would have carried her to the door. Or, if he really did decide to leave her in the car, would he not have handed the sobbing bundle to his driver, or at very least asked the man to keep an eye on her?

Small things like this add up – and they're what you should always look for in deciding whether or not somebody is, like Sutro, trying to pull your leg.

Story Four

Just as incredible in its own way as Sutro's story, but this one is actually true. There are no logical inconsistencies and the questions raised earlier are easily answered. The executive had taken a day off work because it was his birthday. He had access to the garden as part of his tenancy agreement. When there are no contradictions in the story itself, you should never dismiss it just because there are some curious, or unexplained, aspects. You should look for explanation as part of your investigation.

Story Five

You probably thought this one was so fantastic it simply had to be true. But it wasn't. I made the whole ridiculous thing up, as you may have worked out by studying the incidental details.

Forget the coincidence of the wife in the surgery – coincidences do happen and you have to allow for them in physical research. But a grocer lying dead in his own shop which was open (it was a weekday afternoon remember) and none of his customers noticing? That's beginning to sound just a little suspicious, although you might just possibly allow it was a slow day and nobody came into the shop between the time of death and the arrival of the grocer's wife.

But the telling detail is the doctor setting the time of death just minutes before the parrot began to speak. Not even the most expert forensic examination can set time of death with anything remotely approaching that degree of accuracy.

3

Spotting Fake Ghosts

Not all jokers will confine themselves to making up stories. A few of the more energetic will actually try to fake the ghosts. If you're to spot them, it's useful for you to know how to make them.

Let's start with fake séance room ghosts. A séance is a Spiritualist get-together, led by a medium, that's designed to make contact with the dead. Over the years, all sorts of weird happenings have become associated with séances, including:

The appearance of spirits visible to everyone attending.

Overshadowing. The medium's physical appearance seems to change as (s)he takes on the features of a communicating spirit.

Direct voice. Sometimes this term is used to describe spirit messages given by a medium in a voice that is clearly not her own and is believed to be the actual voice of the communicating spirit. But it can also mean voices sounding out of thin air from various parts of the room.

Raps, knocks, sometimes whispers, snatches of music or other sounds that seem to come out of thin air.

Objects moved or even levitated (lifted up). Bells might be rung or musical instruments played by unseen hands.

Brief touches by spirit hands.

Sudden cold associated with the presence of spirits, often accompanied by unexplained breezes.

Ectoplasm, a white substance that emerges from the medium's mouth or other bodily openings.

The appearance of spirit faces or disembodied limbs.

Although many psychical researchers are convinced the various things described have manifested genuinely from time to time, there's no doubt that everything on the list can be, and has been, faked. It's reported that there used to be a factory in Columbus, Ohio, USA, devoted to the manufacture of talking trumpets, ectoplasm and life-size spirit manifestations that could be ordered as séance kits but some of the most convincing fakes have been simplicity itself. Here is what to look out for.

Visible Spirits

Believe it or not, one of the best ways of faking a visible spirit is to dress an accomplice in a white sheet. You'd never believe that would actually work,

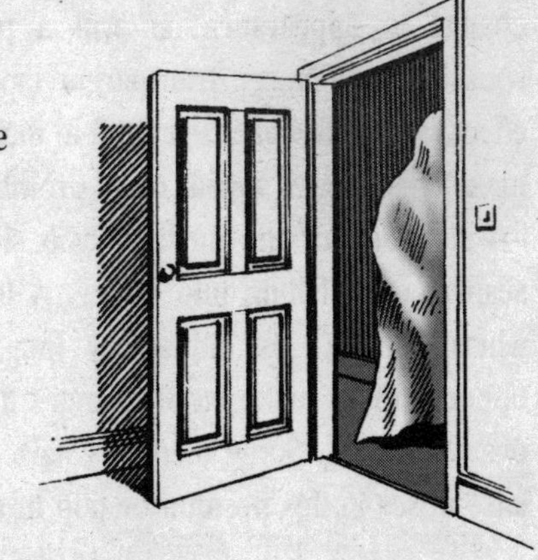

but in the highly charged atmosphere of a séance room, the fleeting glimpse of a white figure can be very convincing.

A variation of the white sheet trick is to have the accomplice simply pretend to be the spirit. Sometimes a little make-up adds to the effect. Bear in mind that the light levels are low during a typical séance and expectations are often high. So if your accomplice gives a good performance as a ghost, many people will take it at face value. One drawback of this variation, however, is that any accomplice runs the risk of being recognised.

There are more sophisticated ways of faking a visible spirit. One is to back-project a slide or suitable movie onto a column of smoke. The smoke might be provided by burning incense (explained as something that 'aids spirit manifestation') lit quite openly when the séance starts. But while methods like this can produce impressive special effects, any serious investigator of your séance will insist on making a search beforehand, with the risk of hidden equipment being found.

Overshadowing

Here again, simplicity is the keynote. Cotton wool pads slipped between the medium's teeth and cheeks will make a distinctive change in appearance, as will a piece of transparent tape squashing the nose. Transparent tape can also be used very effectively to give an Oriental lift to the eyes or stretch the skin to make cheekbones appear more prominent.

Watch out for the medium who slumps forward during the séance, as if falling into trance. A lowered head, particularly where the face is hidden by long hair, presents an ideal opportunity to make facial changes that might be taken for an overshadowing. Some mediums have even been known to don false noses in this position or pop in coloured contact lenses to change the appearance of their eyes.

These very quick disguises don't have to be particularly sophisticated – they have only to pass muster in a very low light. But they do require to be easily and speedily removed, and then hidden, so the medium can return to normal at the end of the séance.

Direct Voice

The form of direct voice that involves the medium speaking is clearly the easiest to fake: all that's required is for the medium to adopt a different accent, or speak in different tones. The interesting thing here is that a number of sitters will accept the sort of phoney voice that wouldn't fool a four-year-old child.

Voices from the air are only slightly more difficult to fake. The best method – because it's completely undetectable – is ventriloquism. A medium capable of throwing her voice can produce the illusion of spirits in any corner of the room. But since ventriloquism is a talent only a few mediums possess, the more usual methods of faking direct voice all involve gimmicks.

In Victorian times, the favourite gimmick was an accomplice and a speaking tube. A speaking tube is exactly what it sounds like – a flexible tube several metres long with a mouthpiece at one or both ends. They were once common on ships, submarines and large shops, where they were used to communicate between one department and another. Even today there are a few about. I saw one used in an old-fashioned jeweller's less than a week ago.

To fake direct voice, Victorian mediums had secret speaking tubes installed, their outlet hidden behind curtains or furniture. An accomplice on the other end, usually in a different room, looked after the 'spirit messages.'

Speaking tubes are seldom used any more, but there's a

variation on the same gimmick that definitely is. Many modern buildings have central heating or air conditioning ducts opening into their rooms. It's sometimes possible for an accomplice to use such ducts in exactly the same way as a speaking tube.

Methods like these are cheap and difficult to detect – if I hadn't told you, would you really have been suspicious of a central-heating grille? But serious professional fakes are perfectly capable of having their séance rooms wired for sound. Hidden speakers, concealed behind pictures or panelling, are linked to a distant microphone. This approach has the added benefit of allowing the accomplice to use creepy sound effects. A second microphone, hidden in the séance room, means there can be interaction with the sitters, so that the 'spirit voice' can engage in conversations.

Raps, etc

A few years ago, the Press reported on a séance held near the ruins of the 17th Century Hell Fire Club in the mountains overlooking Dublin. It had been a remarkable affair, by all accounts. As sitters held hands in the darkness, there were mysterious raps and knocking sounds, eerie whispers, phantom music and, eventually, a hideous moaning sound that terrified everyone present.

The sitters were unanimous that they had experienced some form of spectral manifestation and even the cynical journalist who observed the séance seemed reluctantly impressed. But the medium who conducted the whole affair confessed to me afterwards all the sounds came from a miniature cassette recorder he carried in his pocket. He'd added to the effect by shaking the table with his knee.

The really interesting thing is that the sitters were all aware of the cassette machine. The medium had actually been searched before the séance began. But he blithely claimed that as a psychical researcher, he planned to use the recorder to take notes. The sitters – and observing journalist – accepted the explanation and promptly forgot about the recorder thereafter.

There are even simpler ways of making raps. One of the Fox Sisters, whose spooky experiences led to the foundation of Spiritualism, admitted to producing raps by cracking her joints. It's an annoying habit, but one that can be made to sound really weird in a darkened séance room.

Another useful item is a wooden or plastic spatula. The item is small enough to be smuggled into a séance room, but when snapped against the underside of a table will make a louder noise than you'd ever believe.

Moving Objects

One of the first séances I ever attended was conducted by a medium who'd been thrown out of the S.N.U. (Spiritualists' National Union) for faking a trumpet séance.

A trumpet séance is held in total darkness – not even a dim darkroom light is permitted. An aluminium trumpet with luminous rings painted around each end is placed in the centre of the circle. If all goes well, the spirits will use the trumpet to speak directly to the sitters.

The trumpet séance held by my medium started out rather well. The sitters had been staring at the luminous rings for only a few minutes before the trumpet shivered a little, shook itself violently, then rose

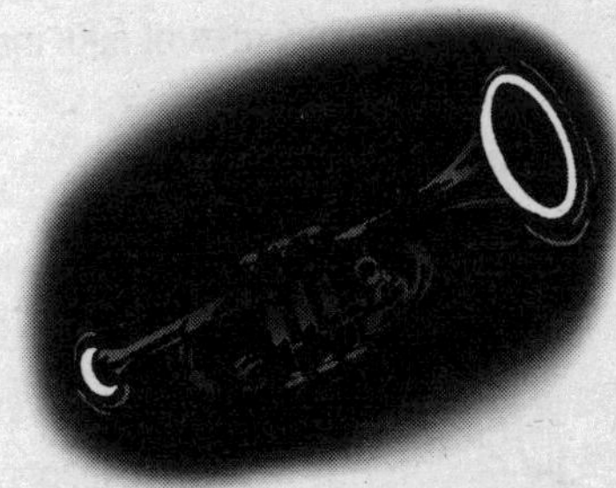

dramatically into the air. Unfortunately a cynic among the congregation switched on the lights at this stage...to reveal the medium on his hands and knees, waving the trumpet above his head.

This is one way to fake moving objects and, like most simple approaches, very effective. The plain fact is very few people have the nerve to switch on the lights at a trumpet séance – the medium will usually make a great fuss beforehand about how dangerous it would be – and consequently such fakery is seldom detected.

Any stage conjurer will tell you a wide variety of objects can be rigged so that they appear to move of their own accord, sometimes using black thread, which is virtually invisible in a darkened room, sometimes calling more sophisticated apparatus into play. There are several trick suppliers on the Internet. In the U.K. I can recommend *www.magictricks.co.uk.*

The major drawback of using rigged objects in a séance is that sooner or later some interfering busybody will insist on examining them beforehand and very few gimmicks will stand up to this. But perfectly genuine objects can still be moved under cover of darkness using a telescopic rod which the medium keeps collapsed in a pocket until needed.

A particularly effective use of the rod arises when all sitters, the medium included, hold hands during the séance. In this sort of situation, use of a rod would seem to be impossible, but there have been exposures of fake mediums who held it in their mouth.

Spirit Touch

Spirit touch, the fleeting sensation of ghostly fingers flitting lightly across your cheek, can be faked in a variety of ways, mostly by way of gimmicks stored near the ceiling, where they are less likely to be discovered in a brief inspection and often concealed in light fittings. (Alternatively, a spirit touch can, like so much else in a faked séance, be provided by an accomplice.)

A small piece of silk, pulled lightly across the skin, feels extremely spooky if you don't know what it is. The effect can be increased by leaving it in the fridge for an hour beforehand. But the spookiest spirit touch of all is that given by a rubber glove filled with iced water. Use just enough water so it takes on the shape of a hand, but remains flexible and wobbly, then tie the end tightly and go to work.

Sudden Cold

The appearance of (genuine) ghosts is often accompanied by a sudden drop in temperature, as if they draw energy from their surroundings in order to manifest. The most usual way to fake this in a séance is to open a window. You'd never imagine anyone would get away with anything so simple and so obvious, but so long as it's done quietly (by an accomplice) most people will accept the sudden chill as a sign that spirits are abroad.

Ectoplasm

Scientists examining genuine ectoplasm discovered its major constituent was hydrochloric acid, suggesting it was somehow spun out of the medium's gastric juices. Sounds like hard work, so some talentless mediums fake it using cheesecloth, a very fine type of muslin. The cheesecloth is tightly rolled, then concealed in the mouth. At the critical moment, the medium spills it out using her tongue.

Disembodied Limbs

Artificial hands, arms and even legs, available at considerable expense from a medical supply shop, have all been pressed into service as séance room 'disembodied limbs.' So has the 'spirit touch' gimmick of a filled rubber glove. A rubber mask on a turnip will provide a convincing head. (Honestly.) An energetic accomplice will have a field day poking them out through curtains or swinging them from hidden thread.

Almost all the above fakes are effective because they are used in a séance room situation where light levels are low, expectations high and close examination of the props discouraged. Producing a fake ghost under strong lights when people don't expect it is a little more difficult, but it can be done. The basic principles were worked out as long ago as 1858 by a retired civil engineer named Henry Dircks, who was trying to figure out a way of presenting a ghost on stage in a theatre.

But while Henry's ideas were basically sound, his designs weren't very practical. Four years after he'd published them, another Henry – Henry Pepper – suggested a redesign. The two got together and the result was an illusion that has come to be called Pepper's Ghost.

Pepper's Ghost requires an actor dressed in ghost costume to be hidden underneath the stage – or to one side of it – unseen by the audience. A large sheet of glass is placed facing the audience, angled in such a way that it reflects an image of the ghost actor. A strong light is played on the actor so that the reflected image becomes strong enough for the audience to see it.

The set-up is largely a matter of trial and error, but once you get it just right, the audience can't see the glass. What they do see is a semi-transparent phantom that can interact with the live actors on stage – a very spooky effect indeed.

In a theatre setting, the audience does not, of course, imagine they are watching a real ghost, but the Pepper illusion can be staged in a private house where it can be used in a séance room to create a ghost or disembodied limb. A flashlight held underneath your face in a Pepper set-up produces a particularly ghastly 'floating head.' The stronger the light, the more solid the head will appear.

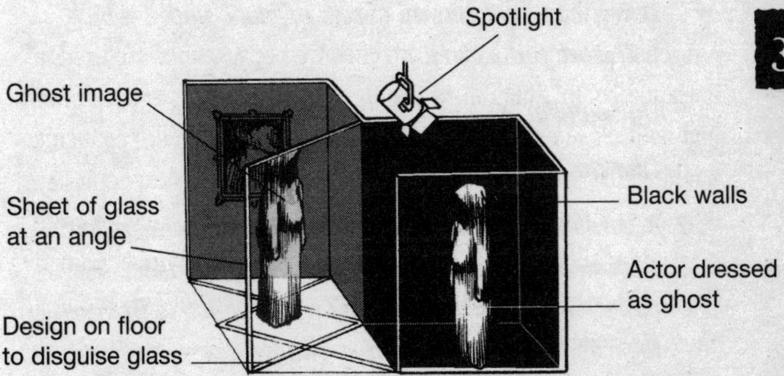

Although the full-scale ghost may require more effort and expense than you'd like, a physics lecturer named David Wall in San Francisco's City College, has figured out a way you can set up an interesting miniature of the effect very easily.

You'll need the following items:

1 *A cardboard box. This can really be any size you happen to have handy, but a shoe box is neat and easy to work with.*

2 *A sheet of Plexiglas, any thickness. The size of the sheet will depend on the size of your box. What you need to do is pick one face of the box which you'll turn into a window and make sure your Plexiglas sheet is big enough to cover it.*

3 *A couple of cardboard strips for use as the window frame.*

4 *A can of black spray paint. (If you can't get this, see if you can find several sheets of black paper, which will work just as well.)*

5 *One candle.*

6 *One candlestick.*

7 *A cardboard tube. The sort they use to send rolled documents and artwork through the post is ideal. Just make sure it's tall enough and wide enough to fit over the candle when it's in the candlestick – and not catch fire!*

8 *A drinking glass or similar small object.*

Start by removing the top of the box, leaving it open. (Oh, and get an adult to help you make this project.) Now cut your window in the front of the box, leaving about 2.5 cm all round as the frame. Glue your two cardboard strips vertically to the inside of the box immediately behind the window frame, leaving enough space for the Plexiglas to slide in and out. Once the glue has dried, but before you install the Plexiglas, spray the inside of the box black (or glue the black paper to the inside for the same effect).

Cut a slot in the side of your cardboard tube running the full length. You're going to have to experiment a little to determine the width of this slot – it should be wide enough so you can see the candle flame from the front, but not too far round the side. Once you've done this, you're ready to rock and roll.

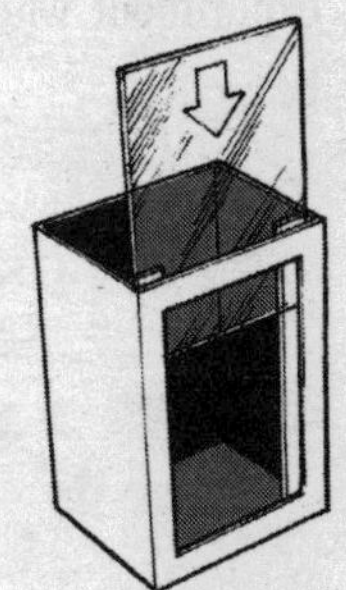

To create your Pepper's Ghost style illusion, you slide the Plexiglas sheet into its cardboard frame so you now have a black box, open at the top, with a Plexiglas window in the front.

Put the candle into the candlestick and light it. Now place the candlestick in front of the Plexiglas window. The reflection that results will give you an illusion of a candle burning inside the black box. Fill your glass with water and set it inside the box in the exact spot where the candle appears to be burning.

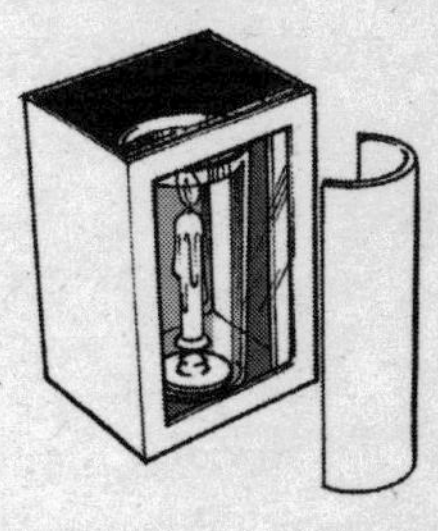

Complete your illusion by hiding the candle in the cardboard tube with the slot facing your Plexiglas window. Assuming you've done everything properly, an audience won't now be able to see your lighted candle (because it's hidden by the tube) but they will see what appears to be a flame burning under water in the glass. Remember, don't leave the candle burning when you're not around.

Since this illusion works exactly the same way Pepper's Ghost does, you might like to experiment with cardboard cut-outs, dolls, toy soldiers and other figures to create miniature spooks. Once you've grasped the basic principle, you can play around by carefully shielding the figures from your audience and illuminating them with a flashlight. You may also have to experiment with the level of your room lighting to achieve the best effect.

When Ghosts Aren't Ghosts

4

Aside from fakes and phoney stories, there are times when perfectly genuine phenomena give all the appearance of a haunting, but don't involve a ghost at all. Take the following case study drawn from the private files of a British ghosthunter:

The story began in the north of England when a couple in their early twenties married and moved into a flat that formed part of a high-rise apartment block. Within a week, strange things began to happen.

At first it was all very low-key. The couple got up one morning and discovered a vase in their living room had been moved from the mantlepiece onto a small coffee table. Their first thought wasn't ghosts, but burglars – the flat was a modern building with no history of any haunting. But when they checked their flat, there was no indication of any break-in, nor was there anything missing. The only mystery was how the vase got from the mantle to the table. They puzzled over it for a while, but eventually put the vase back where it belonged and forgot the whole thing.

Until five days later, that is, when they woke to find all the lights were on in the kitchen, although both could have sworn they'd been switched off the night before. Once again, there was no sign of any break-in or anything missing.

Two mornings later, they found an ashtray that had been left on the coffee table (the same coffee table the vase had crept onto) was now emptied, polished and put away carefully in a cupboard. The next day, some furniture in the spare bedroom had been shifted about. The day after, a table in their little hallway had been exchanged for a hostess trolley that normally sat in their kitchen. Both table and trolley smelled strongly of furniture polish.

Every time anything strange happened, the couple checked and double-checked to find out how the culprit had got in. Since there was no indication of forced entry, they began to wonder if somebody had a key. They considered reporting the whole thing to the police, but decided against it since nothing was missing. All the same, they were now so nervous they had the outside locks changed and put special security catches on the windows.

Not only did these sensible measures make no difference, but the problem actually got worse. More and more things got moved around more and more often until it was a rare morning that they awoke to find nothing touched. On several occasions, they sat up all night to keep watch, but the intruder was too smart for them. On those nights, nothing happened.

It was this more than anything else that convinced them something supernatural was going on. How could any human intruder possibly know when they were waiting for him? They stuck it out for just over six months, with the phenomena becoming more frequent and extreme, before deciding they could take it no longer. By now they were both absolutely convinced they were living in a haunted flat. The only solution seemed to be to get out – and the farther away the better.

They were not a wealthy couple and it was a further three months before they could put their decision into action, but in the event they didn't simply move dwelling, they moved country as well. The husband found himself a job in Ireland and the couple rented a small semi-detached house on the outskirts of Dublin.

The move across the Irish Sea went smoothly, but it was tiring, as was the move in. But all the effort seemed worthwhile. For nearly a month, the couple had peace in their new home. Then their ghost joined them again.

This time there was no gradual build-up. They came down of a morning to find virtually all the furniture in their living room had been moved around. The wife became very upset and the husband made a very weak joke in an attempt to soothe her. He remarked that since the ghost had so much energy, it was a pity they couldn't persuade it to do some housework.

Next morning they came down to find their supper dishes had been washed up and stacked neatly in the draining rack.

From that point on, the ghost became more and more helpful. Washing dishes seemed to be its favourite occupation, but it also emptied ashtrays, dusted, polished and generally cleaned. On one memorable occasion it washed the kitchen floor.

But helpful or not, a ghost is a ghost and the couple were terrified. They'd seen far too many horror movies about haunted houses to be at all comfortable about what was happening to them. Coming down to a supernaturally tidy house each morning, their imaginations ran riot. What sort of creature was doing this? What if it turned nasty? What if it made a mistake...and set the house on fire? Convinced they had to get rid of it, they decided to try exorcism.

Exorcism is a religious ceremony in which a specially trained priest or vicar calls on God's help to get rid of a spirit nuisance. Although seldom discussed, most denominations offer the service, but mainly as a last resort and usually only after a thorough investigation of the phenomenon. The husband went to see his local priest who interviewed both husband and wife on three separate occasions before deciding their distress was both genuine and preternaturally based. He then referred them to an exorcist priest who interviewed them himself and inspected the house before agreeing to act.

The exorcism took place eight days later and lasted just over an hour. It made no difference whatsoever to the haunting.

The couple were actually discussing the possibility of a second move when someone mentioned a psychical researcher who specialised in poltergeists – invisible ghosts who move things about. This seemed a reasonable description of what they'd been going through, so they made an appointment and asked if he would be willing to help.

Although now resident in Ireland, the ghosthunter was born in the north of England like the couple themselves, a fact they found reassuring in their discussions. He explained that before he could offer any advice on getting rid of the ghost, he needed to mount a full investigation to find out exactly what it was. This, he said, would literally mean his moving in to the house to see what was happening for himself. The couple readily agreed.

So the ghosthunter moved in his gear, which included a tape deck and an infra-red camera. When the couple went off to bed, he made himself comfortable in a living room easy chair, turned out the lights and prepared himself for a long night's vigil. Once his eyes adjusted, he could see perfectly well – there was enough light from the street-lamps outside.

Just before three in the morning, the living room door slowly opened. To the ghosthunter's amazement, the wife entered in her nightie and began to tidy up before moving through to the kitchen to wash the dishes. She was sleepwalking.

This was a particularly interesting case of circumstances that suggest a haunting, but have a perfectly natural explanation with no fraud involved. Such situations arise far more often than you'd imagine.

There was, for example, a derelict mansion in Yorkshire which developed a ghostly reputation when motorists driving past caught sight of a phantom figure staring out of an upstairs window. On investigation, the 'ghost' proved to be something even stranger than a haunting. Lightly etched into the glass of the window was the full-length, life-sized figure of a woman, clearly visible from certain angles, but not from others.

The investigators speculated that this may have been a rare natural 'photograph' somehow burned into the glass by lightning while the woman stood next to the window watching an electrical storm.

A much more common phenomenon, known as water hammer, has given many old houses a ghostly reputation. Water hammer arises in central heating systems, particularly old central heating systems, when air gets into the pipes … which it sometimes does after the house has lain unused for a time. Turn the heating on again and loud metallic raps and bangs can occur in empty rooms.

The level of noise generated by water hammer is so high and the sounds themselves so peculiar that anyone unfamiliar with the phenomenon could easily be deceived into thinking they had entered a haunted house.

I experienced an even more spectacular example of a mistaken ghost after I rented an isolated flat on a remote country estate. The environment was picturesque and quiet, but provided me with the most frightening experience of my life.

I was alone in the flat one winter's evening, reading in an easy chair to the light of a standard lamp behind me. The rest of the room – itself quite large – was in gloom. Suddenly, out of nowhere, came the sound of heavy breathing.

I froze in the chair. The noise was quite distinctive, but loud enough to warrant the description 'monstrous.' It sounded for all the world as if some gigantic creature had entered the room and was now lurking in the shadows beyond the pool of light around my chair.

Somehow I found the courage to stand up and investigate. I snapped on the centre light. The room was empty… but there was still something breathing: I could hear it quite distinctly. With considerable difficulty, I eventually tracked down the source of the sound – and discovered it was neither monster nor ghost, but the result of a change of wind direction on the open fireplace. Unusual weather conditions had resulted in a rhythmic down-draught in the chimney that sounded exactly like heavy breathing.

Ghostly lights are something else that can result from natural causes. For centuries, the will-o'-the-wisp – a luminous ghost

occasionally seen flitting across graveyards and over marshland – was believed to be of supernatural origin… or the result of an overheated imagination. Today we know it is neither. Methane gas, produced by decaying vegetation (or in graveyards, decaying corpses) will sometimes ignite spontaneously, causing eerie flames to travel across the ground. Examples of this type underline a lesson that must be learned by every serious ghosthunter. There's a principle of rational thought called Occam's Razor that says when you're faced with a mystery, you must always look for the simplest and most likely explanation. In other words, you're not entitled to call a ghost a ghost until you have ruled out all possibility of a natural explanation.

Even then, as we shall see, some real ghosts aren't exactly what they seem.

5 Grey Ladies

The Oxford English Dictionary defines ghost as 'the supposed apparition of a dead person or animal; a disembodied spirit.' But some perfectly genuine ghosts don't seem to be disembodied spirits at all. One example is the Grey Lady seen frequently at Cleve Court, near Minster in Kent.

Cleve Court was bought by Sir Edward Carson, a well-known Member of Parliament, in 1920 and passed to his wife on his death in 1935. In the early hours of a cold December morning in 1949, Lady Carson was woken up by her spaniel who wanted to go out. Lady Carson pulled on a dressing gown and took the dog downstairs. As she did so, she brushed against a switch and accidentally turned off the light.

Instead of heading for the door, the dog turned tail and ran back up the stairs, whimpering. Lady Carson switched the lights back on again to find there was a young woman in an old-fashioned grey dress coming down the stairs. For a second, Lady Carson thought it was an intruder, then realised she was seeing a ghost. The woman turned on the landing and disappeared into the Elizabethan wing of the house.

Lady Carson was not the only one to see the Grey Lady. Her son Edward began to talk about the ghost when he was just five or six years old, and she was also sighted by four-year-old Patricia

Miller, Lord Carson's great-niece, and five-year-old Diana Colvin, who stayed at the house. When the haunting was publicised in a newspaper, Lady Carson received a letter from a former domestic servant who had seen the Grey Lady as long ago as 1905.

From the various accounts, it is clear that the Grey Lady of Cleve appeared only on the stairs where Lady Carson saw her and a corridor of the Elizabethan wing. She ignored anyone who tried to speak to her, going about her business as if they didn't exist. In this she was very similar to the Grey Lady of Levens Hall, a stately home south of Kendal in Westmoreland.

Levens Hall is an Elizabethan mansion, built about 1586 and the Grey Lady there – one of several ghosts – has been reported right back to the days when a coach and four was the aristocratic way to travel. She used to appear suddenly and startle the horses. In more recent times, there have been reports of her causing motorists to slam on their brakes as they negotiate the driveway to the Hall. When they stop, she promptly fades away. But like Lady Carson's Grey Lady, she never speaks, never communicates in any way, never gives the slightest sign she's aware of those who see her.

This is not what you'd expect from a spirit of the dead. When you start to think about it, you'd imagine that if you find yourself wandering as a ghost, you'd take every opportunity to contact the living, if only to bore them about what happened to you. But the typical Grey Lady ghost never chats, never stops what it's doing, never deviates from a set routine. It will do the same thing over and over for years. If you stand in front of one, it will walk right through you. A member of the Bagot Family, who owned Levens Hall, once accidentally cycled through their Grey Lady without upsetting her in the least.

Grey Ladies are a common type of ghost. In the Church of St Michael and All Angels, a Department of the Environment property at Rycote in Oxfordshire, several people have seen one who glides from a pew to disappear into a stone wall. More startling still is the Grey Lady who occasionally visits the Lion and Lamb in Farnham, Surrey, a café run in converted inn stables which are more than 500 years old. She waits patiently until a member of staff walks up with a menu, then vanishes clean away.

There are several such ghosts at the stately home of Longleat, including one that knocks on bedroom doors. Forde Abbey in Somerset is haunted by a shade that hovers near a table in the Great Hall. Longnor in Shropshire has a Grey Lady. Capestone Hall is home to a line of spectres that descend into a vault beneath the chapel, and a Grey Lady who haunts a garden walk.

You find ghosts of this type throughout the world. In the United States, near Hays, Kansas, for example, 20-year-old Mark Gilbert was working a combine harvester one summer evening when a woman in a long dress stepped in front of the machine. Gilbert braked sharply ... and the woman vanished. Later, when climbing down from the combine, he saw the woman at the bottom of his ladder, surrounded by a haze of blue-white light. Again she disappeared after a brief moment.

Gilbert was only one of a number of people, including a police patrolman, to see the ghost in the long dress. The earliest sighting seems to date back to 1917 when she was spotted by a farmer on horseback.

But the suspicion that Grey Ladies may not be spirits deepens when you realise this type of ghost does not have to be grey at all, or even female. There are many other phantoms that behave exactly the same way as the apparitions we've been examining.

In 1709, for example, the Reverend Thomas Josiah Penston was out and about near Wroxham, on the Norfolk Broads, when he saw an entire phantom Roman army. They marched past in good order, ignoring the astonished clergyman completely and in so doing placed themselves in the category of 'Grey Lady' ghosts.

The Roman legions left Britain in AD 406, so these were very old spooks indeed. But Romans are busily haunting to this day. The last reported sighting I heard about was in the city of Bath in 1988, when a workman was startled to see an ancient Roman walk across an underground chamber then disappear through a wall.

Are we really to believe that when Roman soldiers died in Italy, perhaps in retirement, they rejoined their legion and marched back to the Norfolk Broads? It seems a very odd thing to do, especially when you realise the legions were called home to defend Rome against Alaric's Goths. Surely these old soldiers would stand their ground in case the Goths came back?

The other strange thing about hauntings of this type is that Roman ghosts are as old as you get in Britain. You never hear of a ghostly caveman, or a haunting by a Stone Age hunter. It seems unlikely that all hauntings began with the Romans, so what happened to the ghosts who were around before they invaded? Strange though it may seem, there is some indication they may simply have worn out. There is one well-attested case of a ghost first seen in the 18th century. At that time, it appeared as a woman wearing a red dress. A second report of the same ghost 70 years later described her as wearing pink. By the 19th century, the colour had faded further, leaving her dressed in a grey-white gown. In 1939 she was reduced to phantom footsteps and the swish of her dress. By the time the house she haunted was demolished in 1971, all that was left was a faint sense of her presence.

A friend of mine once saw a Grey Lady type of ghost (actually a Grey Gentleman) while she was a guest in an old manor house. It walked across her bedroom before disappearing through a solid wall. My friend remained sufficiently composed to note that the phantom was walking almost a metre above the floor of the room.

The really interesting thing about this report is that the owners of the mansion later confirmed there had once been a door in the wall at the spot where the ghost disappeared – but it had been bricked up for more than fifty years. Even more to the point, the original floor of the room had once been almost a metre higher than it was now: it had been lowered in Victorian times to get rid of dry rot.

It's not hard to imagine what was going on here. My friend's ghost wasn't really haunting the room where she slept – it was walking across the room as it used to be in an earlier age with its feet firmly on the original floor. And instead of disappearing through a solid wall, it simply used the door that existed in its own time. It's as if somebody *recorded* a Victorian gentleman walking across his bedroom in his nightshirt, then somehow *played it back* to entertain my friend.

The idea that certain ghosts may be natural recordings – perhaps stored in stone or other building materials – has gained a lot of ground among serious ghosthunters. According to some of them, what causes the recording is either constant repetition or intense emotion.

Constant repetition would explain the Victorian gentleman in the nightshirt. Like many of us, he may have followed a set routine – possibly for years – when going to bed. Old abbeys, where monks live ritual lives, are notorious for their hauntings. Intense emotion accounts for the frequent haunting of suicide or murder sites and also goes some way to explain why certain houses feel welcoming while others are cold and offputting.

The British archaeologist Tom Lethbridge, himself a veteran ghosthunter, noted that the sites of hauntings are literally cold: measure them with a thermometer and the temperature is several degrees lower than their surroundings. This led him to his theory of 'ghouls' – limited areas that had somehow been imprinted by strong and usually negative emotions in the past. These did not always produce apparitions so that a typical 'ghoul' was simply a place where you picked up the imprinted emotion and began to feel it for yourself. Thus, for no apparent reason, you would feel angry, sad, fearful or whatever, depending on the imprint.

The effect can be extremely strong. The ill-named megalithic site of Sun Honey in Wales seems to cause gloom and depression in many of its visitors, sometimes lasting for days. It can also be extremely dangerous. There was a haunted room in an Irish seminary that had all the characteristics of one of Lethbridge's ghouls. A depressed student committed suicide by throwing himself out of a window. Thereafter the imprinted emotion caused sensitive visitors to feel they should do the same thing.

It seems fairly obvious that 'ghouls' and 'Grey Ladies' are both different expressions of the same basic process – the natural recording of past events and emotions. Nobody quite knows how one turns into the other, how the imprinted emotion of a ghoul takes on the videotape aspect of a Grey Lady, but one theory suggests that anniversaries may be a factor. Certainly many Grey Lady ghosts appear at the same time in the same place, year after year.

This has led to the interesting speculation that ghosts of this type are related to the orbit of the Earth around the Sun. According to this theory, a Grey Lady is not just imprinted on the stonework of her surroundings, but the position of the Earth in space at the time of the imprinting is an important part of the whole process. When the imprinting is complete, the Earth continues on its orbit and only when it returns to the same point (in exactly one year's time) can the Grey Lady be 'replayed.'

If all this is starting to sound a bit fanciful, it's worth noting there is sound evidence that whatever else they may be, Grey Lady type ghosts simply can't be spirits of the dead. That evidence actually dates back to 1642, a year that saw one of the best-attested hauntings in the entire annals of ghosthunting.

Those of you with an interest in history will recognise 1642 as the starting date of the English Civil War between the Cavalier forces of King Charles I and the Roundhead armies of Parliament under the command of Robert Devereux, 3rd earl of Essex. Although there were earlier skirmishes, the first major clash was the Battle of Edgehill on October 24. A total of 27,000 men took part, including Oliver Cromwell, then just a captain. The battle proved inconclusive, but extremely bloody. Many men died and you can be certain there was a great deal of heady emotion generated while the fighting was going on.

Two months later, the war was still going on, but the focus of conflict had moved away from Edgehill. Thus it was with considerable surprise that a group of travellers, guided by some shepherds, heard drums sounding as they approached the former battlefield.

It was shortly after midnight at the time and when the sound of drums was followed by a hideous groaning noise, the party decided to get out of the area as quickly as possible. But before they had a chance to do so, ghosts appeared in their thousands. Even the Reverend Penston's Roman Legion pales to insignificance when compared with what was happening here. The terrified spectators could see two entire armies, Royalists on one side, Parliamentarians on the other. Within moments they began to fight the Battle of Edgehill all over again.

It was a spectacular sight in full glorious Technicolor® and stereophonic sound. Those watching could hear the terrified squeals of the horses, the clash of steel on steel, the beat of the drums, the roar of the cannon and, everywhere, the screams of the dying. It went on for several hours and the witnesses watched every second of it, an exact replay of the original battle, right down to the point where the King's men withdrew.

The party hurried to the nearby town of Keinton where they swore an account of their experience before the local Minister and a Justice of the Peace. These two worthies, Reverend Samuel Marshal and Mr William Wood, were sufficiently intrigued to want to see for themselves. So the next night they walked out to the battle site, accompanied by a huge crowd from Keinton and several neighbouring parishes. They arrived at Edgehill around midnight. Half an hour later the ghostly armies appeared and fought before scores of witnesses for four hours.

It caused a sensation. Hordes of sightseers turned up the next night and while nothing happened then, the spectral battle was fought again twice the following weekend and on Saturday and Sunday nights for several weeks thereafter.

Talk of what was happening eventually reached the ears of King Charles, then camped at Oxford. Despite the pressures of war, he dispatched six of his best men, led by Colonel Lewis Kirke, to investigate. They reported back that having interviewed witnesses and found their stories convincing, they had gone to Edgehill to see the ghosts for themselves. Not only did the phantom armies appear on cue, but the King's men were able to recognise some of those who took part in the original battle.

And while some of those recognised – like Sir Edmund Varney – had been killed at Edgehill, others were still alive and well. They were known to be elsewhere in England while their phantoms fought the same old fight weekend after weekend.

Poltergeists

When I worked as a newspaper journalist, I was called out to investigate reports of a haunting in a remote Northern Irish farmhouse. The problem had apparently started up several weeks before, but the residents had only recently been prepared to talk to anyone about it.

I arrived to find a thoroughly frightened family. None of them had seen a ghost, but all of them had heard it – or at least heard something. On a regular basis, stones had been tossed onto their corrugated iron roof to the accompaniment of a fearful clatter.

The first time it happened, the parents of the family assumed the stones were thrown by one of their children, although all three vigorously denied it. But then stones began to bounce off the roof while the children were safely inside. Everyone ran out to catch the culprit, but there was no one in sight. After the experience was repeated several times, the family concluded they were being subjected to some sort of supernatural persecution.

The entity involved in cases of this sort is technically known as a *poltergeist*, a German term that translates as 'noisy ghost.' But while there's evidence that some poltergeists may be no more spirits of the dead than Grey Ladies, they are certainly not natural recordings. When the family showed me their roof, I counted 48 stones scattered across it, most of them larger than my fist.

Stone throwing is one of the earliest recorded poltergeist activities. There's an ancient text called the *Annales Fuldenses* that describes how rocks were flung about by an invisible hand in a farmhouse on the Rhine in the 9th century. But unlike the Irish ghost I investigated, the German poltergeist didn't stop there. Rapping noises developed into banging so loud that the walls shook. Worse still, immediately after harvest the farmer's crops mysteriously caught fire.

The Bishop of Mainz dispatched a delegation of priests, heavily armed with holy water and relics, to get rid of the phantom nuisance, but the clerics were pelted with stones for their pains. They were not the only priests to be badly treated by this sort of ghost. According to the monkish historian Geraldus Cambrensus some 12th century exorcists had mud flung at them and holes cut in their clothing.

But these ancient poltergeists were small fry when compared to the haunting of a family home in the Chequerfields housing estate in the English town of Pontefract. The activity that broke out there was among the most spectacular ever recorded in the annals of ghosthunting.

The trouble began on a Thursday in August, 1966, when the only occupants of the house were 15-year-old Phillip Prichard and his grandmother Mrs Sarah Scholes. (The rest of the Prichard Family were on holiday in Devon.) Mrs Scholes was sitting knitting on the settee in the living room when she began to feel deathly cold, despite the fact it was a sunny day. A sudden gust of wind slammed the back door shut and made the windows rattle, but when young Phillip came in from the garden, he reported that the weather was completely calm.

Neither thought very much about it at this stage. Phillip went into the kitchen to make some tea. When he came back out, he found a snowstorm of whitish powder, rather like chalk dust, floating down on his grandmother – who was so absorbed in her knitting she hadn't even noticed.

They looked up to find the source of the powder, having assumed it must be coming down from the ceiling, only to find the air in the top half of the room was completely clear. In fact when Mrs Scholes stood up, her head was above the powder altogether. It seemed to be materialising out of thin air half way down the height of the room.

Mrs Scholes went off to fetch her daughter, Mrs Marie Kelly, who lived across the road. By the time Marie came over to the Prichard house, there was a white layer over the furniture and powder was still falling.

No one, at this stage, had the least suspicion anything supernatural might be going on. Marie Kelly took in the scene and made the practical suggestion that they cleaned things up. She went into the kitchen to get a cloth and found a pool of water on the kitchen floor. As she mopped it up, she noticed another one. And as she mopped that one up, she saw a third forming. Assuming the water was coming up through the lino, she grabbed a corner and pulled it back. The floor underneath was dry.

Enid Prichard, another member of the family who lived next

door, appeared on the scene. As she watched the pools of water forming on the kitchen floor, she sensibly decided to turn off the mains stop-cock under the sink. Unfortunately it made no difference. Mrs Kelly rang the Water Board, who promised to send somebody over.

The man from the Water Board conducted a thorough investigation, but could find no reason for the pools beyond vague speculation that they might be caused by condensation. He went off to report the problem and about an hour later the pools stopped appearing. The women cleaned up the house and everything settled back to normal.

Until seven that evening…

That's when Phillip and his grandmother discovered the work surface beside the kitchen sink was mysteriously covered with sugar and tea. There was a tea dispenser above the sink and as they watched, the button on this activated of its own accord, showering more tea down, then moved in and out, as if an invisible hand was pumping it, until the dispenser was empty.

While they were still trying to come to terms with this frightening development, there was a loud crash from the hall, but when they ran to investigate, nothing seemed to be amiss… except that as they stood there, the light switched itself on.

Determined to discover what had caused the noise, they walked to the foot of the stairs, where they found a houseplant that normally stood at the bottom was now half way up and separated from its pot, which was on the landing above.

Next came a noise from the kitchen. They went to find out what was happening and discovered a cupboard of crockery was shaking furiously, for all the world as if a large animal was trapped inside it. Phillip bravely jerked open the cupboard door and the shaking stopped at once – but a hammering sound started up somewhere else in the house. At this stage the pair decided to get Marie Kelly again.

Mrs Kelly came back to find the kitchen cupboard was shaking again, so violently that the cups and plates inside were rattling.

After a while, things settled down again. Mrs Kelly went back home. Phillip went off to bed. His grandmother, Mrs Scholes, decided she needed an early night as well, but stopped off to kiss Phillip goodnight. The wardrobe in his room was tottering as if someone was rocking it back and forth. Thoroughly frightened by now, Phillip got dressed again and the two of them left the house to spend the night in Marie Kelly's house.

With Phillip and his grandmother safely tucked up in the spare rooms, Marie Kelly and her husband Vic called the police. A small team was dispatched to investigate and a thorough search of the house was carried out, but nothing emerged to explain the bizarre events.

By the time the police left, it was almost midnight. All the same, Vic and Marie Kelly were now so disturbed that they called on a neighbour for help. The man, who was interested in ghosthunting, went with them to investigate. But while they found the house as chill as a grave, there was no further poltergeist activity. They stayed almost two hours before deciding to call it a night. Then, as they were locking the door behind them, there was a crash inside. The Kellys rushed back in to find two oil paintings had fallen from the living room wall and a wedding photograph had been slashed from end to end.

Two days later, the Prichards returned from their Devon holiday and heard the whole sorry tale. As most people would, they found it hard to believe. But when they asked about the rapping sounds, there were three loud bangs, immediately followed by a rattling of the windows and a blast of chill air throughout the house.

And that was that. The weird phenomena stopped as abruptly as it started. The family gradually settled down. Memories faded. Everything returned to normal.

Then, two years later, it started up again.

The first hint of trouble came when Mrs Scholes began to hear mysterious sounds in the house. Since no one else had noticed them, this was put down to imagination at first. But then came a loud crash heard by Jean Prichard. Two counterpanes were stripped from beds upstairs and flung down into the hall. Plant pots were violently upended, leaving soil everywhere.

It was the beginning of a nightmare. Jean Prichard got up in the night to discover something swaying and rustling on the landing. She switched on the light and a paintbrush flew past her face. Then a bucket of wallpaper paste was flung against the wall. A roll of wallpaper on the landing was rearing up like a snake. A carpet sweeper launched itself into the air and whirled around as if brandished by an invisible hand. The terrified woman dropped on all fours and crawled back into her bedroom. A second roll of wallpaper hit the door behind her. Jean Prichard screamed.

The scream woke her husband Joe and their children Phillip (who'd seen the ghostly activity two years earlier) and his sister Diane. Paintbrushes and other decorating materials began to fling themselves around. One brush struck Diane on the shoulder.

In Diane's bedroom, a wooden pelmet was torn from the wall and flung through the window. Joe Prichard slammed the door to keep whatever it was inside. The family could hear frantic bangs and thumps in the room.

It was the start of a major haunting by Mr Nobody, as the Prichards named their ghost. Typically, drumming noises started up around bedtime and ornaments levitated or were thrown across the room. All the lights in the house would go off as the mains switch was thrown. This happened so often that Jean Prichard actually taped it in the ON position. Half an hour later the lights went out again. The switch was off and the tape had vanished.

The local vicar was called in to discuss the possibility of an exorcism. While he was there, candlesticks levitated from the mantlepiece before falling on the floor and, next door in the living room, the contents of the china cupboard were tipped violently onto the carpet – without, however, breaking.

After he left, a huge shadow appeared on one wall and the place became chill. The lights went out yet again and a heavy hallstand with an electric sewing machine on it moved of its own accord to knock over Diane Prichard and pin her to the stairs. When she was freed by her parents and put to bed, the bedclothes were pulled off her and flung into a corner of the room. Her mattress then levitated, tipped her onto the floor, then fell on top of her. When she got her bed back to normal, it happened again, and again, and again … four times altogether throughout the night.

It went on and on in the days ahead. A grandfather clock was thrown downstairs. Knocks and raps continued. Mysterious scents filled the air. Chairs were tipped over, drawers pulled out and emptied, objects flew about, lights went on and off. Something with enormous teeth took a bite out of a sandwich. A jug of milk was poured over a cynical visitor. The contents of a refrigerator were strewn about the room.

Perhaps the most frightening incident of all was when a pair of enormous hairy hands appeared around a door. These turned out to be fur gloves, worn by something invisible… and huge.

Eventually the ghost began to show itself. The Prichard parents were in bed one evening when the door of their room opened to reveal a dim, hooded figure that disappeared the moment they switched on the light. Then the haunting spread to the neighbouring house – the Prichard's home was semi-detached – the owner there, Mrs May Mountain, turned from her kitchen sink to find a tall, hooded man in the black habit of a monk standing behind her. He seemed perfectly real and solid until he disappeared before her eyes.

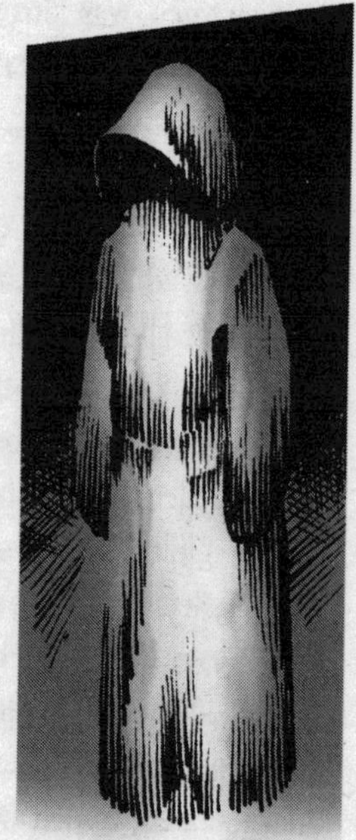

6

The Prichards finally got rid of their unwelcome visitor using a method that would have done justice to a Dracula movie – they hung garlic cloves around their house. All phenomena stopped at once and the monkish Mr Nobody never appeared again.

The Pontefract Poltergeist seems to have been a disembodied spirit – investigation later revealed that a Cluniac monk had been hanged in Tudor times on the spot where the Prichard home now stands – but other, equally spectacular cases have proven to be nothing of the sort.

Just a year after the Pontefract case, for example, a German lawyer named Sigmund Adam began to experience problems with his office lighting. He had a relatively modern system of strip lights installed, but they kept failing with monotonous – and inexplicable – regularity. The problem grew so bad that he installed a special meter in an attempt to find the cause. It showed the lights themselves were not at fault – massive electrical surges were simply blowing them.

But what was causing the mysterious surges? Adam's office was in Rosenheim, a small town south west of Munich, so he placed a call to the *Stadtwerke*, the local electricity company. They sent an engineer to test the power lines, but he found nothing amiss. When the lights continued to blow, a direct cable was installed...still without solving the problem.

Herr Adam decided to take matters into his own hands. He bought his own generator and replaced the strip lights with ordinary bulbs, but these moves made no difference either.

Then he found the lights were the least of his problems. A massive phone bill arrived, showing the calls from his office had increased dramatically – too dramatically for Adam to stomach. This time he called the phone company and complained. When the usual reassurances failed to satisfy, the phone company agreed to install a special monitor. To everyone's astonishment, it showed someone was dialling the Speaking Clock for hours on end, four, five and even six times a minute. In some cases the calls were being placed faster than a human hand could operate a telephone. It was all completely impossible, but since the calls originated from Herr Adam's office the phone company insisted he was responsible for the enormous bill. While the lawyer was still reeling from this bad news, the poltergeist activity started.

A local reporter got wind of the story and published a report on the 'Rosenheim ghost.' At once, the story was taken up by the national Press. Among those who read the account was one of Europe's leading ghosthunters, Professor Hans Bender of the Institute of Paranormal Research at Freiburg in Germany.

Bender called Adams and asked permission to investigate. The lawyer was only too happy for anything that might help solve the multiplying mysteries. Professor Bender travelled to Rosenheim and quickly confirmed something very spooky was going on. Lights swung for no apparent reason, pictures turned on the wall, a heavy filing cabinet was moved by unseen hands.

But Bender was convinced this was no ghost. Everything that happened seemed connected to a teenage girl named Anne-Marie Schaberl, who'd joined the company two years previously. The power surges that blew the lights only occurred when she was in the building. Poltergeist activity broke out when she entered a room, died away when she left. He even observed that when she walked along a corridor, the overhead lights would begin to swing back and forth of their own accord.

Once Bender filed his report, Adam promptly fired the girl. She found employment in another office ... and a poltergeist haunting began there as well. When she went ten-pin bowling the electronic equipment malfunctioned. She took a mill job, but left when a fellow worker was killed by machinery that went haywire as Anne-Marie walked past.

Cases like this have led many professional ghosthunters to conclude poltergeists have less to do with the spirits of the dead than with the mysterious powers of the human mind. Bender tested the girl. While she remained relaxed, she showed no sign of any peculiar abilities, but once she became emotional, her ESP (extra-sensory perception) scores went through the roof. Bender decided Anne-Marie was causing the various phenomena without realising she was doing it – a process technically known as psychokinesis.

Even apart from the Rosenheim case, many poltergeists seem to follow certain people about, particularly young people just entering their teens. The theory is that they are caused by bottled-up emotions that can't be expressed any other way. The teenagers concerned don't know they are creating a poltergeist, but they seem to be doing so just the same. Very often a haunting can be stopped by finding the 'carrier' and trying to solve the problems that are making him or her unhappy.

But while some poltergeists may be weird examples of the terrifying powers of mind over matter, this explanation doesn't hold good for them all. There have been many cases that seem to be caused entirely by disembodied entities and a few, possibly including the Pontefract case, where a genuine spook draws energy from living people in order to throw things around.

Spirits Of The Dead

7

For all the fakes, natural recordings and emotional poltergeists that haunt the annals of psychical research, there still seem to be a few spirits of the dead around. In fact, the earliest ghost ever recorded – by the Roman orator Pliny the Younger in the 1st century AD – falls into this category.

Pliny's report concerned a haunted house in the Greek city of Athens. So many people complained of seeing a ghost there that the landlord found himself with a property difficult to rent. Then along came a Greek philosopher called Athenodorus. Since Greek philosophers aren't stupid, he figured he might get the house very cheaply. That turned out to be an accurate assessment of the position. He rented it for a pittance and moved in at once.

It would probably be unwise to assume Athenodorus did not believe in ghosts – most Greeks of his day certainly did – but on the first night in his new residence he got so involved in his work he forgot all about it. The ghost didn't forget about him. Around midnight it announced its presence with a ghastly rattling of chains.

Athenodorus looked up to find he had been joined by a spectral figure, an old man with a tangled beard. The apparition, heavily fettered with chains, beckoned him with a bony finger. (It's interesting that the details of this 2,000-year-old report have turned up again and again in subsequent accounts. The spectral figure of the old man, the clanking chains, the beckoning finger might all have been taken from Charles Dickens' *Christmas Carol* (but for the fact it was written 1,800 years later).

The laid-back Athenodorus ignored the ghostly summons for as long as he could, but eventually found the noise of the chains so disturbing that he got up and followed the spectre. It led him out of the house and into a garden, then walked into the middle of some shrubs and promptly disappeared.

Athenodorus decided the phantom was trying to tell him something. He convinced the city authorities to dig up the shrub bed and a chained skeleton was unearthed. Pliny records that once it was reburied by a priest in sacred ground, the haunting stopped.

It's difficult to see how this sighting could be explained away as a natural recording or some sort of emotionally generated effect and there seems to be no motive for deliberate fraud. Plainly, the ghost was aware of Athenodorus (and others before him). It wanted something and was able to show what that was. It behaved like an intelligent entity. The critical factor is that it communicated. This is one of the most important pointers towards a spirit of the dead.

London's most famous historical haunting – the Cock Lane Ghost – shared the ability to communicate, even though it was never actually seen. The trouble started in the Cock Lane

(Smithfield) home of Richard Parsons, a clerk at Saint Sepulchre's Church.

Parsons was a widower, living with his children and sister-in-law, Fanny Lynes. In November, 1759, he went away on business and Fanny, a very nervous woman, asked his eldest daughter, 10-year-old Elizabeth, to sleep with her for company.

Elizabeth moved into the bedroom and, after a few nights, scratching and rapping noises started, keeping them awake. When Parsons came home again, he thought the noises were probably made by the cobbler next door. Then Fanny Lynes went down with smallpox. Parsons moved her into a nearby house to prevent the rest of his family catching the disease. She died on February 2, 1760.

But before Fanny died, the noises in Parsons' house got so bad he called in a carpenter to see if there was something trapped behind the panelling. When it was removed there was nothing to explain the noises. Beginning to suspect something supernatural was afoot, Parsons asked the Reverend John Moore, assistant preacher at St Sepulchre's, to come and investigate.

The Reverend Moore decided he was dealing with a ghost and suggested it might talk to him using a code of one tap for yes, two taps for no and a scratching sound if it was displeased about anything. In this way, the spirit told Moore and Parsons that it was the ghost of Fanny Lynes.

At this point the story took a dramatic turn. The ghostly Fanny claimed she hadn't died of smallpox at all – she'd been murdered by a man named William Kent, poisoned with arsenic, which he put in her beer.

Parsons believed the story, but may have been a little prejudiced. He owed William Kent £20 and Kent was suing him for repayment. The Public Ledger newspaper published a sensational account in January 1762. Kent read it and was horrified to learn he had been accused of murder by a ghost. He went to see the Reverend Moore, who suggested he visited the haunted house and hear the ghost for himself.

Kent took him up on the suggestion. Along with the doctor and apothecary who had attended Fanny Lynes during her last illness he headed for Parsons' house. When he got there, the whole place was like a carnival. Elizabeth's bedroom was packed with people hoping to hear the ghost. Elizabeth herself was in bed with her younger sister.

At first nothing happened – Elizabeth said there were too many people about. The Reverend Moore cleared the room. The spirit began rapping and everybody crowded in again.

"Are you the spirit of Fanny Lynes?" asked the Reverend Moore.

One knock – yes.

"Were you murdered by William Kent?"

One knock – yes.

"Was anybody else involved in the murder?"

Two knocks – no.

"Thou art a lying spirit!" shouted William Kent. But nobody believed him.

Word went round like wildfire and the whole of Cock Lane jammed with sightseers. A committee was set up to investigate and concluded the ghost was a fraud. The ghost responded by making a curtain spin on its rod and producing whispering noises. A satirical pamphlet was brought out, probably by the poet Oliver Goldsmith. A satirical play about the ghost was staged at Covent Garden.

William Kent mounted a lawsuit against Parsons. The judges were not impressed by all the talk of ghosts and sentenced

Parsons to two years jail with three stands at the pillory where he was pelted with rotting vegetables by passers-by.

The apparition that confronted Athenodorus might seem at first glance to be a Grey Lady type of ghost while the raps and noises in Cock Lane could lead you to believe a poltergeist was at work. But the one thing in both cases that marks these ghosts as spirits of the dead is that they were able to communicate. The Athens phantom knew Athenodorus was there, signalled to him, then showed him where the bones were buried. The noisy ghost in London was able to set up a code and pass messages back and forth.

It's this element of communication that sparked off the entire Spiritualist movement and created generations of mediums who believe – often with good reason – that they can receive messages from spirits of the dead.

This is what happened. In 1847, an American farmer named James D. Fox moved with his wife and family into a haunted house in Hydesville, New York. Haunted or not, things were quiet enough until March, 1848 when banging noises started in the walls. It was a timber frame house and the family thought the sounds were due to bad weather.

But on the last day of March, they found out differently. At this time, everybody slept in the same bedroom, in two separate beds – parents in one, two daughters in the other. As the parents were coming to bed, the raps started again and one of the daughters, 12-year-old Kate, suddenly snapped her fingers and said loudly, "Mr Splitfoot, do as I do!" To everyone's astonishment, the raps changed to finger-snapping noises.

Kate's 15-year-old sister Margaretta promptly joined in the game by clapping her hands and shouting, "Do as I do." The finger-snapping changed to the sound of hands clapping.

The girls thought somebody might be playing a joke on them – the next day was April 1, April Fool's Day. Their mother wasn't so sure and thought she'd try a test. She asked the ghost to rap out the ages of her daughters, convinced that a joker wouldn't know them. At once there came 12 raps (Kate's age) followed by 15 (for Margaretta.) Then the ghost rapped out the age of a third Fox child who had died…

Like the Reverend Moore in Cock Lane, Mrs Fox suggested setting up a communication code – two raps for yes, one for no. Then she began by asking if the raps were being made by a human. There was absolute silence. Perhaps by a spirit? Two enormous raps came in answer, so loud that the entire house shook. After an hour or so of careful trial-and-error questions the family had learned that the ghost was the spirit of a man who'd been murdered in the house at the age of 31.

An excited Mrs Fox ran out to spread the word among her neighbours and some 14 of them crowded in to listen to the ghost. One of them – a man named William Duesler – suggested working out a more elaborate code so the ghost could communicate properly. This was duly done and the spirit seized the opportunity to tell the little congregation that he was a pedlar named Charles B. Rosma who had stayed in the house five years earlier. He had been attacked and murdered there for the sake of $500 he was carrying and his body buried in the cellar. (The basic story was later confirmed. A maidservant named Lucretia Pulver recalled that a pedlar *had* stayed in the house five years before, but disappeared abruptly. Later still, human bones were dug up in the cellar.)

All this proved to be the start of something big. As news of the spirit messages spread, hundreds of people flocked to the Fox farmstead to hear them for themselves. When Kate was sent to stay with her sister in Rochester, she started communicating with a dead relative named Jacob Smith. (The sister, Leah, soon found she could talk to spirits too.) Margaretta went to stay with her brother in Auburn and raps broke out there. Meanwhile, the original pedlar was still rattling the walls – and producing ghastly gurgling noises – at Hydesville.

Then suddenly spooks were breaking out all over. A 16-year-old called Harriet Bebee came to hear the raps that Margaretta seemed to be producing in Auburn and was followed home by something that caused more raps there. When the Fox family moved to Rochester, they received a spirit message that said, 'Dear friends, you must proclaim this truth to the world. This is the dawning of a new era. You must not try to conceal it any longer. God will protect you and good spirits will watch over you.'

Before long all sorts of things were happening – tables turned and tapped messages with their legs, objects moved of their own accord, spirits played musical instruments. The first-ever official Spiritualist meeting took place on November 14, 1849, in the gloom of Rochester's Corinthian Hall. In a matter of months, ghosts were communicating right throughout America.

The craze reached Britain a short time later – Queen Victoria was amused to hold séances in Buckingham Palace – then spread across Europe. Although the high excitement has died down, thousands of Spiritualist meetings are held throughout the world to this day.

But it seems that spirits of the dead can do more than communicate. There is strong evidence that they can take over people's bodies as well. One of the most interesting cases of this phenomenon – known to ghosthunters as possession – involved a 13-year-old American girl named Lurancy Vennum.

There was something wrong with Lurancy because in the summer of 1877 she suddenly fell down in a fit at her home in Watseka, Illinois. She seemed to recover without ill-effects, but from that time on further aberrations occurred. She took to falling into sudden trances. In some of them, spirits seemed to take her over.

Lurancy's parents called in a local doctor, who decided to use hypnosis as a cure. While deeply hypnotised, Lurancy claimed her symptoms had all been caused by evil spirits. Then she announced there was a spirit in the room at that moment – someone named Mary Roff – which she would allow to possess her for a time as proof. The next morning, Lurancy woke up claiming to be Mary Roff.

On the face of it, the most likely explanation was that Lurancy was either faking it or mad, but it quickly turned out neither was the case. First of all, it transpired there really was a Mary Roff –

or at least there had been. Mary was a local girl who had died in 1865, about a year after Lurancy was born.

Then, when Lurancy was taken to Mary's home, she recognised all the Roff relatives and was able to call them by name, even though Lurancy had never met any of them before. She also recognised Mary's old schoolteacher.

It quickly became clear that Lurancy 'remembered' dozens of incidents from Mary's childhood. She was able to describe them in considerable detail – so much so, in fact, that the Roff family became convinced they were talking to their dead daughter in somebody else's body and asked to have Lurancy live with them.

The Vennum family were understandably reluctant until 'Mary' told them that 'the angels' would only let her stay in Lurancy's body for three months. After that, an agreement was struck and Lurancy/Mary moved in with the Roffs.

There she stayed, week upon week, never once saying or doing anything to leave the Roff parents in the slightest doubt she was their dead daughter. Then, exactly three months later, Mary abruptly disappeared and Lurancy, her old personality and memories intact, walked back home. Veteran ghosthunter Richard Hodgson, of the Society for Psychical Research, thoroughly investigated the case and concluded it was genuine. He believed there were only two possible explanations. One was that Lurancy had developed a second personality with astounding psychic powers – something he thought extremely unlikely. The other was that the spirit of Mary Roff, wandering the world after her death, had temporarily taken over the body of Lurancy Vennum.

The idea that spirits of the dead can wander the world underpins the most common theory of ghosts. The fact that spirits like the Fox Family's pedlar, the Cock Lane rapper and America's

Mary Roff are able to communicate seems to give the theory substance. But a good ghosthunter has to be careful. Because there are two other types of phantom that can and do communicate … but have nothing at all to do with spirits of the dead.

Phantoms Of The Living

An extraordinary thing happened to me one winter's night some 30 years ago. I'd just gone to bed and was in the process of falling asleep when I found myself standing in a narrow country lane several hundred metres from my house. I had no idea how I'd got there, no memory of leaving my bed, yet there I was, bathed in moonlight, wearing my pyjamas and a very startled look. A chill wind was whistling through the trees.

Thoroughly bewildered, I started to walk back to the house – and found myself instantly in bed again to the sound of a loud metallic clang.

I lay there, heart pounding, wondering what on earth had happened. But eventually a sensible explanation dawned on me. I hadn't been *falling* asleep – I'd actually *fallen* asleep and dreamed I was outside. The dream had been so vivid I'd mistaken it for reality. Which seemed so reasonable, I settled down at once and quickly forgot the whole thing. Until a few weeks later …

This time I woke up in the middle of the night needing the loo. The bathroom was just down the corridor from the bedroom. I climbed out of bed, walked across the room and discovered the bedroom door was locked.

I couldn't understand it. I never lock the bedroom door, nor did my wife. I was certain neither of us had locked it the night before.

Yet the door wouldn't open. Then, as I reached out to try the handle, I noticed something really, really weird. My fingers weren't gripping the knob – they were sinking into it.

I glanced across the room and the weirdness got worse. There was a bearded man lying in the bed beside my sleeping wife. After a moment, I realised the bearded man was me! For a moment, nothing made sense. Then it dawned on me I had somehow got up and crossed the room *while leaving my body behind*. I walked back to the bed and lay down. As I did so, I sank into my body which was already lying there.

You might imagine an experience like this would have unnerved me. In fact, it seemed the most natural thing in the world. But I still needed the loo. So, having realigned myself with my body, I got up again. When I reached the door, I still couldn't work the handle and my body was still lying on the bed.

Six times in all I went back to the bed, realigned with my body and tried to persuade it to get up. Six times it lay there like a corpse. On the fifth occasion, I didn't just reach the bedroom door, but walked right through it. On the sixth, I walked right through the (closed) bathroom door as well. I felt perfectly solid and normal, but I was passing through solid objects like a ghost.

Finally, on the seventh attempt, I somehow managed to persuade my body to come with me to the bathroom, have a pee then tramp back to the bed.

I didn't know it at the time, but I'd had what's technically called an Out-Of-Body

Experience, or OOBE for short. They're a lot more common than you'd think. Surveys have shown a quarter of all students in Britain have had at least one OOBE and the occurrence is even more common among the really clever ones – Oxford undergraduates showed a rate of 34%. In America, almost half (46.6%) the readers of a mass circulation magazine reported that they'd left their bodies. It's something that seems to be particularly common at puberty.

As I discovered, when you have an OOBE it feels exactly as if you're wandering around like a ghost with your physical body left somewhere behind. But is that actually what's happening, or are you simply dreaming or perhaps hallucinating? Odd though it sounds, there's a wealth of evidence that in some OOBEs at least, you really do become a ghost without the inconvenience of dying first.

Take, for example, the case of the English schoolteacher – I'll

call her Lesley, since she doesn't want her real name revealed in print – who told me of her own experience after I'd given a lecture on OOBEs at a conference centre in Dartmoor.

It happened during a warm spell when Lesley's school had planned a trip to the mountains for pupils and teachers. Lesley badly wanted to go on the trip, but decided against it since she was on a course at the time and had to attend lectures on the same day. As it happened, she found she couldn't concentrate on the lectures. It was an unpleasant, humid day and she spent the entire time daydreaming about her students and colleagues in the cool air of the mountains.

The day of the trip was a Friday. The following Monday, Lesley turned up for school as usual. In the staff room at lunchtime, another of the teachers asked her how she'd enjoyed her day in the mountains. Lesley sorrowfully told him she hadn't gone. Her colleague looked at her in astonishment, "Of course you went," he said. "I spent most of the afternoon talking to you."

It seems that during the time Leslie spent daydreaming about joining her friends on the school trip she'd somehow sent a ghostly double of herself into the mountains – and this phantom appeared real enough and solid enough to convince one of her colleagues she was really there. What's more, it proved capable of holding a conversation Lesley herself knew nothing about.

It seems that schoolteachers are particularly prone to this sort of thing. In 1845, a Livonian languages teacher named Emilie Sagee was sacked from the School for Young Ladies near Riga because she was upsetting her pupils, who kept seeing two of her.

A phantom Emilie Sagee might be standing next to the real one by the blackboard, or sitting quietly in a corner watching the first one work. There were even times when Emilie was indoors while her ghost strolled around the school grounds. And it kept on happening. She lost no fewer than 18 jobs because of it.

Phantoms of the living can travel vast distances very quickly. Eighteen years after Emilie Sagee lost her job, an American manufacturer named Wilmot was on board the *City of Limerick* in the mid-Atlantic when he dreamed that his wife visited him in her nightdress and kissed him. The following morning he woke up to teasing from his cabin-mate, who claimed he'd seen a lady visiting Wilmot in the night.

When Wilmot got home to Bridgeport, Connecticut, his wife promptly asked him if he'd received a visit from her in the night. She had been worried by reports of shipwrecks and tried to find out if he was safe by imagining herself flying over the ocean and finding his ship. She felt she'd somehow come on board the *City of Limerick* and found his cabin.

Intrigued, Wilmot asked her for more details and she was able

to describe both the ship and the cabin with considerable accuracy. She knew Wilmot had occupied the lower bunk. The man in the upper bunk, whom she described accurately as well, looked straight at her as she entered the cabin, but she was so relieved to discover her husband was all right that she went across and kissed him.

Although there was no spoken communication in this case, there seems little doubt that Mrs Wilmot's ghost somehow visited the *City of Limerick* while she was very much alive. While there she was seen by her husband, who thought he was dreaming, and his cabin-mate, who knew he was not.

A more recent example of the same type of case arose in America in 1957 when an Illinois woman named Martha Johnson decided to find out if her mother was all right. Like Mrs Wilmot, she imagined herself visiting her mother who lived close on a thousand miles away in Minnesota.

Like Mrs Wilmot on the ship, Martha 'saw' her mother at work in the kitchen. Martha stood beside a cupboard and watched her until her mother became agitated, turned and looked directly at her.

The fact that something more than imagination was at work here is borne out by a letter which Martha's mother wrote the following day. It stated, "It would have been about ten after two, your time. I was pressing a blouse here in the kitchen. I looked up and there you were at the cupboard just standing smiling at me. I started to speak to you and you were gone. I forgot for a moment where I was. I think the dogs saw you too. They got so excited."

Here again, it seems that someone's ghost managed to travel far from its owner's body while the owner was still very much alive.

Even aside from the statistical reports mentioned earlier, well-attested cases of this type are more common than you'd think. In 1886, the Society for Psychical Research published *Phantasms of the Living* which detailed 350 of them. In 1951, Sylvan Muldoon and Hereward Carrington added another 100 in their book, *Phenomena of Astral Projection*. Three years later, Hornell Hart was examining 288 cases in the *Journal of the American Society for Psychical Research*. Another psychical researcher, Robert Crockall published nine more books of case histories between 1961 and 1978. Author John Poynton added 122 cases in 1978.

I even generated a few case studies myself. After my experience with the bedroom door, I set up several experiments that used hypnosis to trigger OOBEs. In one, a teenage girl left her body and travelled to read a message left for her in a house 100 miles away. She failed to do so 'because it was too dark' but was able to count the number of words and accurately describe the paper and handwriting.

In another series of experiments involving a middle-aged businessman, the subject was able to travel as a ghost to Bombay in India where he discovered to his horror that his favourite restaurant had been demolished. Later investigation confirmed this was absolutely correct, as was his observation of a newly built wall. When his phantom went on a much shorter trip to the house next door which he'd never physically visited, he was able to

describe the interior and furnishings of several rooms in detail and even observed the owner going about his business.

Cases like these have convinced experienced ghosthunters they can't automatically assume any phantom that communicates must be a spirit of the dead. And indeed, there is evidence that even some mediumistic messages may originate from the living rather than the dead.

In 1921, a ghosthunter named Dr S.G. Soal decided to investigate a well-known medium of the day, Mrs Blanche Cooper. He set up a series of regular séances over a period of several months and kept careful records of the results. In one of early sessions, a spirit named Gordon Davis came through.

As it happened, Dr Soal actually knew a Gordon Davis – they had been old school pals. But they had lost touch during the First World War when Davis joined the Army. Two years after the war ended (and a year before he began the séances with Mrs Cooper) Soal received news that his friend had been killed by a shell in the trenches in France.

It quickly became clear that the spirit was the same Gordon Davis. He chatted to Soal about their school days and mentioned details that could only have been known to the two of them. One telling detail convinced Soal this was a genuine communication from beyond the grave. Davis asked if he remembered their last conversation. Soal racked his brains, but could not… until Davis reminded him it had been the result of a chance meeting on a train and gave an accurate account of what had been said.

With his bona-fides established, Davis told Soal his only worry now was his wife and children. He described the house where they were living, complete with details like the 'five-and-a-half' steps that led to the front door, the dark tunnel nearby, the landscape pictures inside the house, the ornamental bird on the piano and the brass candlesticks on the downstairs shelf. He remarked mysteriously that it stood on only 'half a street.'

When the series of séances ended, Soal filed away his notebooks and thought little more about the communications. Then, three years later, he accidentally discovered Gordon Davis's widow was living in Southend-on-Sea. The spirit messages came flooding back and it struck him this could be the perfect opportunity to find out how accurate the information about the house might be. Soal arranged to pay a call – and brought his notebooks with him.

With growing excitement, Soal discovered detail after detail checked out. The first thing he noticed was that the house was on an esplanade facing the sea. There were no houses opposite, so it could be said to be situated in 'half a street.' There was a dark tunnel next to it, an enclosed alley leading to the back gardens.

Soal counted six steps up to the front door, but one was very thin compared to the others, which would explain why the spirit of Gordon Davis had jokingly remarked there were only five and a half.

Inside, the house was exactly as described. Soal saw the landscape pictures, the ornamental bird on the piano, the brass candlesticks and other furnishings. But he also saw his old friend Gordon Davis, who had not been killed in the war at all.

Astonishingly, Davis had no knowledge of his 'spirit messages' and had only moved into the house with his wife in 1922, a year after the séances with Blanche Cooper were finished.

But communications from 'ghosts of the dead' that turn out to be spirits of the living are not the weirdest phenomena ghosthunters have to face. There are two even more bizarre categories of phantom you'll need to take into account. The first is examined in our next chapter.

Phantoms Of Time

It was a hot August afternoon in the year 1901. Two respectable Victorian ladies, Miss Charlotte Anne Elizabeth Moberly and Miss Eleanor Frances Jourdain, were on holiday together in France and decided to visit the Palace of Louis XIV in Versailles.

Both ladies were schoolteachers. Miss Moberly was principal of St Hugh's Hall at the University of Oxford, a very prestigious educational establishment. Miss Jourdain had founded her own girls' school in Watford and rented a flat in Paris as a sort of finishing school headquarters for her pupils.

The two women met earlier in the year and Miss Moberly was so impressed by Miss Jourdain that she invited her to become vice-principal of St Hugh's. Miss Jourdain liked the idea, but before making any decision, she suggested she and Miss Moberly should stay together in her Paris flat for a time to see how they got on. Miss Moberly readily agreed.

As a result, each of them arranged a three-week holiday and sailed for France. Since they were both interested in history, they decided to visit various historical sites together. Most of these were in Paris. One, the magnificent Palace of Versailles, was only a 16-kilometre train ride away. On August 10, the two companions took that train.

Despite its name, the Palace of Versailles is not one building but many, set in extensive formal grounds. The original residence was built between 1631 and 1634 as a hunting lodge for Louis XIII, but it was Louis XIV who turned it into an immense and extravagant complex. It was the seat of monarchy and home to the Court until the French Revolution in 1789. In 1901 (and indeed today) it was one of the country's major tourist attractions. It is enormous by the standards of any age, so the Misses Moberly and Jourdain had a lot to see.

The two companions spent most of the day in the main palace, touring its many rooms and galleries. When they eventually got tired, they rested in the Salle des Glaces and discussed how best to spend the remainder of their visit. Around four in the afternoon, Miss Moberly suggested they visit the Petit Trianon.

The Petit Trianon is one of the minor palaces at Versailles. It was designed by the architect Ange-Jacques Gabriel and built in 1762 as a private residence for Louis XV, his family and their guests. But its most famous resident was the ill-fated Marie Antoinette, who was given the house by her husband, Louis XVI in 1774. Visit it today and you'll discover an elegant, well-proportioned building surrounded by beautifully kept gardens.

The Petit Trianon lies about a kilometre and a half north west of the main palace. The two ladies consulted their guide map and set off to find it. They arrived eventually at the Grand Trianon, a companion building … and lost their way.

Later, it turned out their mistake was simple – they reached the main drive (which was deserted at the time) but went straight on instead of turning right. This took them into a narrow lane that ran approximately at right angles to the main drive. Miss Moberly noticed a building on the corner of the lane and a woman shaking a cloth out of a window. She expected Miss Jourdain would ask the woman for directions, but Miss Jourdain did not. Miss

Moberly decided her companion knew where she was going and followed her up the lane.

They walked north for a while, chatting together about England, before taking a right turn that brought them past several buildings. The doorway of one was open and through it they could see the bottom of an elaborate staircase, but since there was no one about, they didn't like to go in.

Soon they found themselves facing a choice of three paths. They consulted their map but couldn't decide where they were supposed to be. There were two men on the centre path and the ladies walked across to ask them for directions. At this point, a hint of strangeness enters the story. Although both ladies were later to refer to the men as gardeners, Miss Moberly actually described them as two 'very dignified officials, dressed in long, greyish-green coats with small three-cornered hats.' This is not, of course, typical Victorian clothing. The three-cornered hats in particular would mark it as 18th century costume.

The officials were not the only ones whose clothing looked out of place. There was a small cottage over to the right with a woman and girl standing in the doorway. Both wore dresses that seemed the better part of a century out of date.

Despite these peculiarities, Miss Jourdain asked the men for directions and was told to go straight on. But there was something so odd about the way the men spoke that she asked again – and received the same answer.

As the ladies walked on, they were both seized by an

inexplicable feeling of depression and loneliness. Miss Jourdain described it as an oppressively 'heavy dreaminess.' The path they were on ended in a T-junction and as they left it, the sense of oppression grew much worse. There was a small wood in front of them with a circular garden kiosk overshadowed by trees. The grass around it was covered in dead leaves, as if high summer had suddenly turned to autumn. According to Miss Moberly, everything suddenly looked unnatural. The trees beyond the kiosk took on the flat, lifeless appearance of a tapestry. Something peculiar had happened to the usual play of light and shade. Everything became deathly still.

Miss Jourdain was afraid. There was a man in a heavy black cloak seated on the steps of the kiosk, a slouch hat pulled down to conceal his features. He looked slowly towards them and they saw an evil face marked with the ravages of smallpox. His dark eyes stared right through them.

Anxious to avoid the evil-looking man, they took a turn to the right. There was the sound of running footsteps, but when Miss Moberly turned she could see no one on the paths. Then, as if out of nowhere, a man appeared. He was handsome, with the look of a gentleman about him, yet somehow gave the impression of having stepped out of an old print. He called out to them in a strangely accented old-fashioned French that they should go to the right, not the left. The ladies did so, but when they turned to thank him, the man was no longer there...but again they heard the running footsteps.

The two *Mesdames*, as the man had called them, crossed a little bridge and skirted a narrow meadow overshadowed by trees. There Miss Moberly saw a youngish woman in an old-fashioned pale green dress, sketching. They carried on up some steps onto a terrace when a young man emerged from a house and offered to show them where they wanted to go. They went with him and quickly arrived at the front entrance of the Petit Trianon where they wandered around the rooms in the wake of a lively French wedding party. Their sense of oppression finally lifted and they took a carriage back to their hotel for tea.

At this point, the visit to Versailles seemed strange, but not *that* strange. But things changed when the two ladies got around to comparing notes and found that the woman sketching, seen so clearly by Miss Moberly, had not been seen by Miss Jourdain at all. Yet, reported Miss Moberly, "it was impossible that she should not have seen the individual: for we were walking side by side and walked straight up to her, passed her and looked down upon her from the terrace."

"Do you think the Petit Trianon is haunted?" Miss Moberly asked her companion.

"Yes, I do," said Miss Jourdain promptly.

But was it? The two ladies again visited Versailles together in the summer of 1904 and found it inexplicably changed. The trees they saw had gone, as had the kiosk, the bridge they had crossed and an ornamental cascade they'd seen. It seemed as if everything had been radically modernised, but when they talked to officials at the Palace and consulted their guidebooks, they discovered no modernisation had taken place since their last visit.

Following a grim intuition, they decided to consult the history books...and found that the Petit Trianon they'd visited in 1901 was not at all as it was in their own day, but exactly as it *had been* at the time of Louis XVI. Old prints even enabled Miss Moberly to recognise the woman sketching in the pale green dress – she looked eerily like Louis' queen, Marie Antoinette.

But this was no haunting by spirits. The entire place was changed when the two ladies first visited it. Nor was it any sort of natural recording. The 'ghosts' of the Trianon were aware of their visitors and capable of talking to them. What seems to have happened was that Miss Moberly and Miss Jourdain somehow took a trip through time.

This theory sounds too outlandish to take seriously until you realise there's substantial evidence that this sort of 'time slip' has happened to other people.

In October, 1957, for example, three teenagers from the HMS *Ganges*, a Royal Navy shore training establishment, went on an exercise that took them close to the Suffolk village of Kersey. They heard bells and followed the sound. This brought them close to the church at the southern end of the village, but as they climbed a fence, the bells suddenly stopped.

They followed a dirt track and eventually emerged in the village itself. But all three 15-year-olds saw at once that something was wrong. The church had disappeared and the village was completely deserted. There were no cars or vans, no bicycles, no electricity or telephone wires, no radio or TV aerials. The only living things were a few motionless ducks beside a stream. And everything was deathly silent. Like the ladies at Versailles, the boys at Kersey felt a sudden depression.

They took a drink from the stream to quench their thirst, then set out cautiously to explore. The haunting sensation of something badly amiss persisted. Although it was autumn and the world around Kersey was turning gold, the trees here were just breaking bud, as if it were the beginning of spring. There was only one shop in the whole place – a butchery with skinned ox carcasses hanging inside. But the place was filthy and covered in cobwebs, the carcasses literally green with age, as if the butcher was long gone.

English villages are famous for their pretty gardens. In this one there were no gardens at all, not so much as a window box, in fact. When the boys looked into the few dark, small, old (and very dirty) houses, there were no curtains at the windows and scarcely a stick of furniture inside.

In the absolute stillness, the boys had the sensation they were being watched. They began to walk faster, then broke into a run and left the village at top speed. As they did so, the sound of bells came again, the church reappeared and there was smoke in the air above Kersey where there had been none before.

Some careful investigation by members of the Society for Psychical Research determined that the boys had wandered into Kersey not as it is in modern times, but as it was 500 years earlier, in the middle of the 15th century. They speculated that the time slip may have taken the boys to a period when the village was temporarily deserted because of plague.

Another, even more recent time slip occurred in the winter of 1973 when a Cambridge schoolteacher, Mrs Jane O'Neill, went on a visit to Fotheringhay Church in Northamptonshire.

Everything seemed entirely normal. The church had several interesting features and Mrs O'Neill spent some time admiring a splendid picture of the Crucifixion behind the altar on the left side of the church. It had, she said afterwards, an arched top. Inside the arch was a dove with its wings following the curve.

Back in her hotel room some hours later, a friend named Shirley happened to read aloud from an essay that mentioned a particular type of arch. "Sounds like the arch of the picture I saw in the church," Mrs O'Neill remarked. But Shirley looked at her blankly. "There's no picture in the church," she said.

Shirley's reaction worried Mrs O'Neill. While she didn't want to disbelieve her friend, she was quite certain of what she'd seen, so she rang the local postmistress, a woman who arranged flowers in the church every Sunday. The postmistress confirmed there was no picture of the Crucifixion, although there was a board behind the altar with a painting of a dove.

A year later, Jane O'Neill went back to Fotheringhay Church. The outside was exactly as she remembered it, but when she went inside she knew at once she was in a different building. It was much smaller than the Fotheringhay she'd visited before. This time there was no painting of the Crucifixion.

9

Thoroughly bewildered by now, she got in touch with a Northamptonshire historian. From him she learned that there had actually been two Fotheringhay churches on the site. The first was a very ancient building that was demolished in 1553. The second, and present, building had then been erected on the original foundations. Intrigued, Mrs O'Neill began research into the original church … and discovered the building she'd entered in 1973 was the one that had been demolished more than four hundred years earlier.

While time slips obviously don't happen often, the case studies in this chapter – which are only a few of the many available – show that they do happen sometimes. And if one happens to you, the people you encounter in the different time-line can easily be mistaken for ghosts ... which they are, in a sense, but not as returned spirits of the dead.

But odd though they are, time slips aren't quite the weirdest thing a good ghosthunter has to take into account. That category is filled by a phenomenon examined in the next chapter – the artificial ghost.

How To Make A (Real) Ghost

In 1976, there was an outbreak of curious phenomena at the home of a Kent housewife named Pamela Masters. It started quietly enough with objects moved out of place in the night, but progressed slowly to a point where mysterious drawings appeared on the walls and a coffee cup was wrenched from the hands of the person drinking from it.

At this point, it seemed like a typical poltergeist haunting, right down to the fact there was a teenage girl in the house, Mrs Masters' 19-year-old daughter Karen. But then things took on a
10 very peculiar turn. Mrs Masters saw a phantom figure in the house, then later, a different phantom in another room. Thereafter both phantoms continued to appear at intervals and were seen by a total of six witnesses.

Mrs Masters recognised the phantoms – their photographs were all over the house. They were Paul Michael Glaser and David Soul, two American movie actors world famous for their starring roles in the television detective series Starsky and Hutch. Karen Masters was their biggest fan. She'd collected so many of their pictures that her mother had been complaining for weeks.

Both Glaser and Soul were very much alive at the time of the haunting (and are still alive at time of writing, so far as I'm aware). But the case was hardly typical of phantoms of the living. Neither actor knew of the Masters family, nor had any reason to 'visit' the house where they lived. What seemed much more likely – and much more strange – was that Karen Masters had obsessed about the actors so much she had somehow created their ghosts, complete with attendant poltergeist activity.

Is it really possible to create a ghost in this way? There seems little doubt that it's possible to create a poltergeist that doesn't involve the appearance of a phantom. The way to do so was discovered by a British psychologist and ghosthunter called Kenneth Batcheldor.

Batcheldor was interested in table-turning, something that first happened during the Spiritualist craze in Victorian times. Instead of messages from mediums, some séances featured tables that would twitch, jerk, rattle about, move and sometimes even levitate, apparently under the influence of spirit visitors. But the trouble with table-turning, so far as Batcheldor was concerned, was that it didn't happen any more. When the Victorian craze died down, Spiritualists turned their attention to other ways of communicating with the dead and séance tables went back to a much more stolid existence. Batcheldor decided to see if he could get them moving again.

To this end, on April 25, 1964, he started the first of a series of some 200 experimental sessions involving family, friends and himself. The group met regularly and would sit around a table with their hands resting lightly on it. None of the sitters thought of themselves as a medium and most didn't believe in spirits. What they were engaged in was a simple scientific experiment to see if they could duplicate the reported table movements of Victorian times. It proved a trial of patience. A total of 120 sittings produced no results at all. But the remaining 80 got very interesting indeed.

Batcheldor reported that nothing much happened in the first few sessions beyond very slight table movements that could be accounted for by involuntary muscle twitches. Then, on the eleventh sitting, the table rose clear of the ground and floated in the air – something well beyond any muscle pressure exerted on the top.

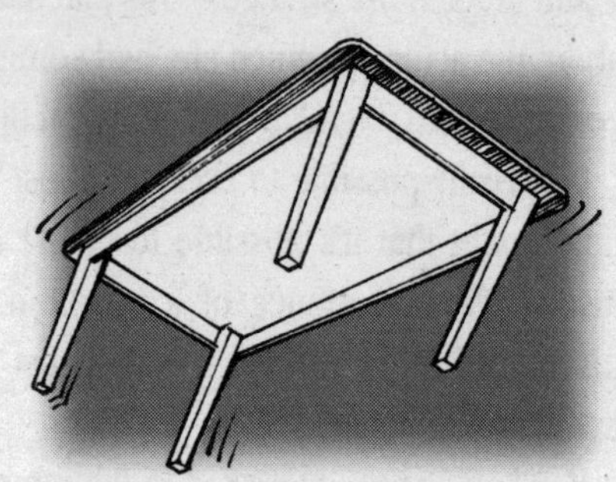

By the time Batcheldor's experiments were finished, he'd not only produced table levitations, but confirmed them using pressure-sensitive electrical contacts and photographed them using infra-red light. He'd also produced a variety of other séance room phenomena associated with spirits – sudden drops in temperature, phantom lights, ghostly touches and so on. But the really interesting thing was the way he produced them.

Bear in mind Batcheldor wasn't a Spiritualist or a medium. He was a scientist interested in producing certain effects and then finding out what it really was that caused them. But he quickly discovered it was no use setting up a sitting with rigid scientific controls: when you tried that, nothing happened. What you had to do was sit with no controls whatsoever until something peculiar happened.

Without controls, you couldn't rule out the possibility somebody might be cheating or that what was happening had a perfectly rational explanation. But that was okay. You just kept holding sessions without controls until you could be fairly sure of something odd happening at each one. Then you brought in a tiny measure of control.

You might, for example, hold your first sessions in pitch darkness where you couldn't see what anybody was doing. Then, when the phenomenon was established, you might introduce a very dim light. The dim light wasn't much, but it was your first control.

Batcheldor found that when a control was introduced, the phenomenon fell away, but if you were patient, it gradually came back again as your sitters got used to the new conditions. When it was firmly re-established, you introduced your next control.

By introducing scientific controls in very small, easy stages, Batcheldor was eventually able to duplicate the most spectacular of the Victorian phenomena under the most stringent conditions. Eleven other groups used the same method to produce equally spectacular results, including one I took part in myself.

There seems little doubt that something paranormal was going on, but equally little doubt that it had nothing to do with spirits. It looked very much as if the groups gradually trained themselves to produce results under what amounted to laboratory conditions. In essence, each group was creating effects – table turning, raps, cold breezes, light touches, etc – normally associated with a ghost.

Just a year or two after Batcheldor finished his experiments in 1969, a Canadian group under the leadership of Dr George and Mrs Iris Owen decided to go a step further and see if they could create not just the phenomena associated with a ghost, but the ghost itself – an entity that could communicate with them just as real spirits of the dead are supposed to.

They began by creating a character, exactly as a novelist might create the hero of a story. In this case the hero was a minor nobleman named Philip, who lived at the time of the English Civil War. His story was tragic. He fell in love with a beautiful gypsy girl named Margo, but his wife Dorothea found out about the affair. In a brutal act of vengeance, Dorothea had Margo accused of witchcraft. Margo was tried, convicted and burned at the stake. Philip was so distraught he committed suicide by throwing himself off the battlements of his family home, Diddington Manor.

It has to be stressed that, with the exception of one small detail, none of this was true. Philip never lived, nor did Dorothea or Margo. All three were figments of the group's collective imagination. The story was a complete fiction as well, with no historical basis at all. The only element that had any foundation in fact was Diddington Manor, which actually existed.

With agreement reached on the character and his story, the group then began to meet regularly in an attempt to bring Philip to life (so to speak) through a series of séances. They managed to get hold of some photographs of Diddington Manor, which they pinned around the walls. Then they sat in silent meditation, thinking long and hard about Philip and his unhappy fate. This went on for several months, during which absolutely nothing happened.

Thoroughly fed up with the whole affair, the group decided on a more relaxed approach. Instead of the intense concentration, they simply chatted about Philip and the experiment. On one occasion, they even sang a few songs.

The new approach paid off. After just a few more sessions, there was a phantom rap on the table. Like the Fox family before them, the group promptly set up a code and soon the 'spirit' was communicating freely. They asked for its name and found they were talking to 'Philip', the fictional character they had created. When questioned, Philip told his life story exactly as they had made it up.

This was weird enough, but worse was to follow. From the first few hesitant raps, the phenomena got stronger until Philip was able to move the table – on one occasion it was reported that he danced it up the steps of a public platform. Then he began to add details to his story that went beyond the fictions created by the group. His descriptions of Cromwellian life were so vivid that the group began to wonder if they had really made him up after all. Some members began to suspect they might have read a genuine life story then forgotten it, but used the details quite unconsciously to create their fictional Philip.

The suspicion grew to such an extent that intensive new research was undertaken. But it failed to solve the growing mystery. It seemed that Philip really was just a fictional character. Yet he was now busily expanding his story well beyond anything the group had originally worked out.

Eventually, he began to supply historical details of life in Cromwellian England that none of the group members knew, but were checked out afterwards and found to be accurate …

The work done by the Canadian group shows it is possible to create a ghost that communicates by raps and poltergeist phenomena. An experiment I set up in 1997 with a British group shows that 'ghosts' of this type can manifest even more fully.

Over an intensive five-day period, the group worked hard to

create a fictional Saxon priestess, exactly as the Owen group created Philip. With the story agreed and firmly in place, a ceremony was conducted to find out if the entity could be persuaded to communicate. Unlike the Canadian experience there were no raps or knocks. Instead, one of the group members fell into trance and began, like a Spiritualist medium, to speak with the voice of the Saxon priestess. When questioned, the entity fed back the fictional story the group had created.

But even this does not represent a limit to the way artificial ghosts may manifest. The distinguished French academic and traveller, Madame Alexandra David-Neel, reported that while camping in Tibet, she was visited by a young local artist who had a special devotion for a particular Tibetan deity. For years he had meditated regularly on the deity and painted innumerable portraits of it. As he entered the camp, Madame David-Neel could clearly see the phantom figure of the deity standing behind him.

She was so taken by the phenomenon that she began to make inquiries and discovered to her surprise that many Tibetans were quite familiar with phantoms created by intense visualisation or meditation. There was even a Tibetan word for it – such phantoms were known as *tulpas*.

Thoroughly intrigued, Madame David-Neel decided to see if she could manufacture a tulpa herself. She settled into a routine of visualising a fat and jolly little monk in a brown robe, rather like Friar Tuck in the story of Robin Hood. At first it was difficult, but eventually the visualisations grew more and more vivid until something curious happened – she began to get glimpses of the monk around her camp even when she was not visualising him. Then other members of her party began to 'see' the monk as well: he seemed so solid that her herdsmen actually took him for a real person.

It seemed as though Madame David-Neel's tulpa experiment was a resounding success, but then, very gradually, things started to go wrong. The phantom monk, by now a regular visitor to the camp, started to lose weight and take on a sly, malevolent appearance. Worse still, when Madame David-Neel tried to dismiss him, he refused to go. It took her six months of hard work and deep concentration before she managed to 'dematerialise' him again.

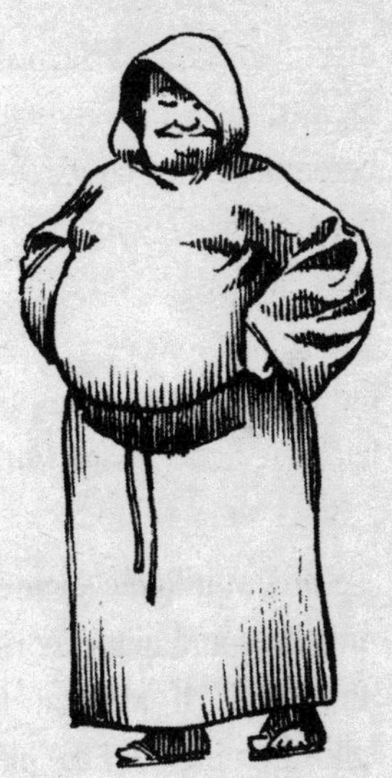

How To Hunt For Ghosts

So now you know some ghosts can be fakes, some ghosts can be mistakes and many more have nothing at all to do with spirits of the dead. If all that hasn't put you off, it's time to start ghosthunting. And the place to start is with your Ghost Box.

You have made up a Ghost Box, haven't you? If not, go back to the beginning of this handbook and put one together now, otherwise the rest of this chapter isn't going to do a lot for you.

Still with me? Good. The first thing I'm going to teach you is dowsing. The *Concise Oxford Dictionary* defines dowsing as 'the search for underground water or minerals by holding a Y-shaped stick or rod which dips abruptly when over the right spot.' Which is accurate enough, except that you don't need the traditional Y-shaped stick. You can get just as good results from a pendulum or a set of L-shaped rods – and both of them are a lot easier to use.

Easiest of all are the rods. Take the ones you made from coathangers out of your Ghost Box and look at them with pride. Simple though they were to construct, these are about the finest, most sensitive, easy-to-use dowsing rods you could own. My old American friend Steve Peek, who fought in the Vietnam War, once told me that rods exactly like these were used by the G.I.s to detect landmines in preference to the sophisticated electronic equipment issued by the US Army. They literally bet their lives that the rods would do a better job.

They'll certainly do an excellent job in detecting water. To use them, hold each one loosely by the short leg, like this:

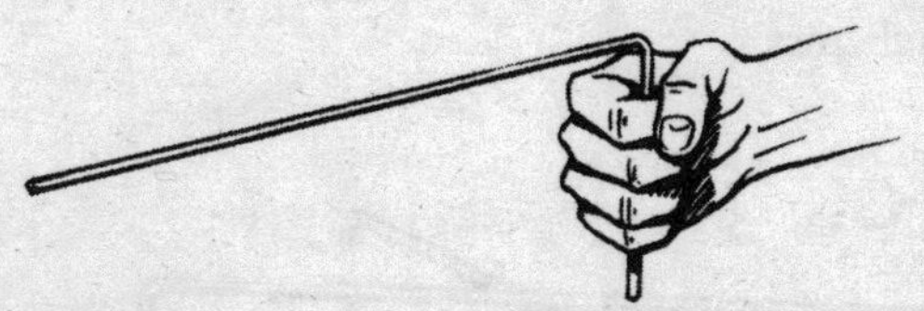

The rod should be able to swing easily, left and right, so a light grip is important.

Dowsing takes a little practice, but not much and it's my experience that while not everybody can manage it, three or four out of every five people can get results using rods like these. The best place to start is on any piece of land where you know there's an underground stream or even a water main. Ideally, you should know its exact location. It's important that it's running water – an experienced dowser can pick up an underground pool, but running water is far easier for a beginner.

If all this seems a tall order, you can always go find an open stream – you're only practising after all. But you'll have to try your hand at hidden (underground) water eventually.

Start out some distance from where you know the water runs and hold your two rods parallel, like this:

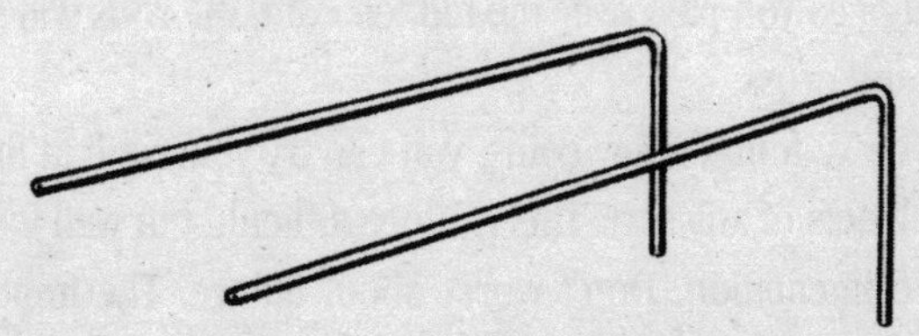

Remember to grip them loosely, then tuck your elbows in to your sides and walk slowly in a line that will take you across the watercourse, roughly at right angles. As you cross the stream or pipe, you'll find that the two long arms of the rods swing slowly inwards and cross.

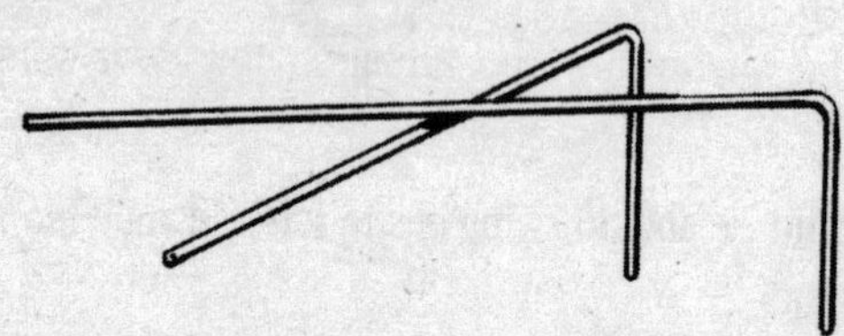

You don't need to do anything for this to happen. You don't even need to concentrate. Just hold the rods loosely, walk slowly and they'll cross of their own accord.

Your next step is to try to detect water where you don't know its location in advance. The simplest thing is to go to a friend's house and try to detect where his water main comes into the building. Afterwards you can check how accurate you were.

When you have had a little practice with running water, you can move on to metals and minerals. Have a friend hide a coin somewhere underneath a large rug or carpet, making sure there are no visible clues to its location. Take your rods as before, but this time hold another coin of the same denomination in one hand along with the rod. Walk across the carpet in a tight grid pattern. Once again, as you pass over the hidden coin, the rods will swing inwards and cross.

Once you've found a few coins, you can try your skill at finding hidden objects of any sort. This is more difficult, but well worth a little experimentation. Don't worry about failure. The important thing is to keep practising until you're relaxed and confident. At that point, you can start using the rods to hunt for ghosts.

All you really need is intention. Go to any site where a haunting has been reported. Hold the rods exactly as you did when dowsing for water and metals. Then make a mental decision that you are now going to look for traces of a ghost. That mental decision is the whole trick. It locks you in on the faint traces hauntings seem to leave behind.

Just as you did when you were learning to dowse for water, it's a good idea to start by using the rods at places where you definitely know a ghost was sighted. Once you can get a reaction there, you can go on to track ghosts in areas where you don't know the exact location. Witnesses to the original sighting can confirm whether or not you've got it right.

Your ghost pendulum will do the same job as your ghost rods, but in a slightly more sophisticated way. You use it by setting it swinging in a shallow arc.

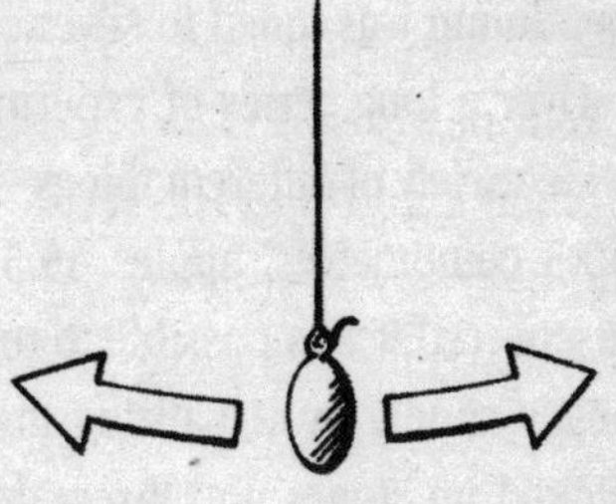

Let it continue to swing as you walk from place to place. You know you have a dowsing reaction (like the rods crossing) when, at a given spot, the pendulum stops swinging to and fro and then starts to describe a circle.

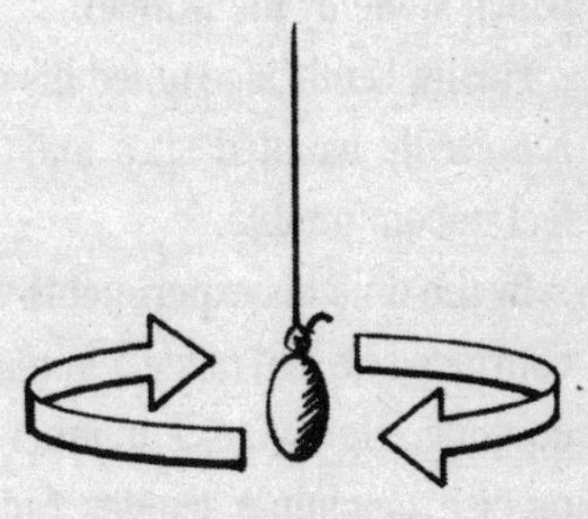

11

Again like the rods, this is something that happens of its own accord. But using a pendulum properly takes preparation. The rods are an all-purpose dowsing instrument, but the pendulum is more specific and has to be tuned in.

The British archaeologist Tom Lethbridge – the same one who theorised about 'ghouls' – was the ghosthunter who discovered how to tune a pendulum. He had the idea it might be useful to find out if different lengths reacted to different things. To test his theory, he made a long pendulum and wrapped the string around a pencil so that the length could be varied easily.

He started by putting a silver dish on the floor and swinging his dowsing pendulum over it. Then he varied the length of the string until the pendulum suddenly started to circle. He measured the string 56 centimetres and concluded that a 56-centimetre long pendulum was tuned to silver.

Over a long series of experiments, he discovered lengths for a wide variety of different things – copper was 76 centimetres, grass 40.5 cemtimetres, apples 45.5 centimetres and so on. He even discovered it was possible to tune the pendulum to emotions like anger simply by visualizing them clearly. He and his wife Mina picked up stones and threw them against a wall. The pendulum could be tuned to detect which stone was thrown by the man and which stone by the woman.

Finally, Lethbridge tuned his pendulum to ghosts by heading for reportedly haunted sites and dowsing in areas that made him feel uncomfortable.

By the time his experiments were finished, Tom Lethbridge was convinced he had made a fundamental discovery about pendulum dowsing. He wrote a number of books in which he gave the precise pendulum lengths for various substances. Lethbridge's discovery wasn't what he thought. It turns out that while different pendulum lengths let you dowse for different things, the lengths themselves are not the same for everybody. What you have to do is tune your own pendulum.

You can, of course, experiment over a whole range of materials, but as a ghosthunter, you really only need to tune your pendulum to the length that detects ghosts. Follow Tom Lethbridge's example by searching out some haunted sites. Walk around until you find an uncomfortable spot or use your rods to detect the likely location of a haunting. Roll the string of your pendulum around a pencil until it is only about 15 centimetres long, then set it swinging. Gradually shorten or lengthen the string until you get the circular dowsing reaction. Make a note of the length and check out that it works in other haunted sites.

The weird thing is that while you can only use the rods to detect ghosts if you are on a haunted site, you can use the pendulum to detect ghosts (or rather the haunted sites themselves) by holding it over a map!

If this strikes you as completely impossible, I'd be the first to agree. But the fact remains that it works. More to the point, it's not all that difficult. Lethbridge not only pinpointed hauntings in this way, but also made a habit of finding hitherto undiscovered prehistoric remains. (He maintained his academic reputation by concealing his methods until after his retirement.)

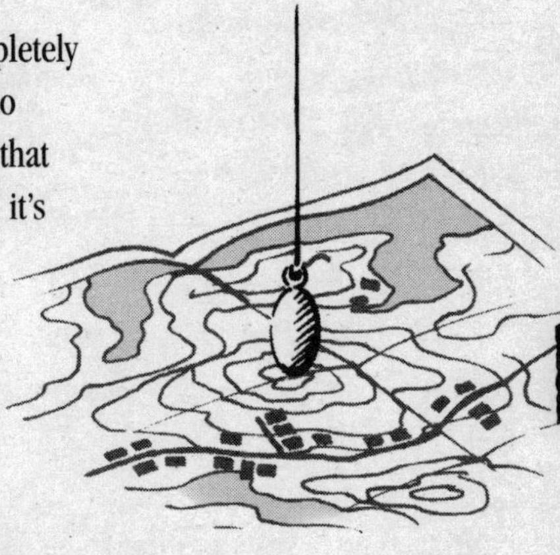

To do the trick, you make a firm decision that you're dowsing for ghosts, then swing your pendulum over a large scale Ordnance

Survey map. Follow a grid pattern until you get the circular reaction. It's possible to use smaller scale maps, but you can't really pinpoint haunted sites this way, since the area your pendulum circles will cover many square kilometres. When Lethbridge made a discovery using map dowsing, he always checked it in the field – a habit you might usefully employ.

Talking To Ghosts

If you ever find yourself leafing through the many civil service records of Ancient China, you may stumble on mysterious references to something that translates as 'the flying pencil.' Like the rulers of most ancient civilisations, the Mandarins of China were not opposed to talking with spirits – not to mention acting on their advice – and the flying pencil was the way they did it.

I saw the flying pencil in action for myself when investigating a Cornish Celt who claimed she was in contact with a spirit guide. Challenged to prove it, she found herself a stiff-backed notebook and a pencil stub. Then she sat down in a comfortable chair, pencil poised over the notebook which was open on a little table beside her. She took several deep breaths, then her eyes slowly drooped as she sank into trance.

After a few minutes, her hand began to move. Moments later, the pencil was indeed flying as she filled page after page of the notebook with a handwritten message from her guide.

I can't remember what was in the message now, but I do recall that the handwriting looked nothing like the psychic's own. In some places the words were joined up together, likethesewordsarejoinedtogether, as if the pencil was moving too fast to separate them.

The process is known outside China as 'automatic writing.' Psychical researchers are divided on whether the messages really arise from ghosts or erupt from the unconscious mind of the person holding the pencil, but experience shows that experiments with automatic writing can produce interesting, and sometimes downright eerie, results. You have to be psychic to develop automatic writing, so it's not the sort of thing an inexperienced ghosthunter should try. This is what typically happens:

After a period of time – which varies greatly with the individual – the psychic's hand will twitch. Then the twitch turns into a jerk before the hand describes a larger movement, causing the pencil to scribble on the paper. Given time and practice, probably over a series of sessions, these apparently random movements begin to produce words.

Since this method of automatic writing is difficult to develop and works for only a few specially talented people, attempts were made by ghosthunters many years ago to automate the process. The result was a device called a planchette, which became popular during the Victorian Spiritualist craze.

In its Victorian form, a planchette was a heart-shaped wooden board a little larger than a man's hand, attached to castors so that it could move freely in any direction. Near the point of the board was a hole through which you could push a pencil. Some psychics found the device made it easier to receive spirit messages than straightforward automatic writing.

Even more popular than the planchette is the ouija board where a pointer can sometimes be persuaded to spell out spirit messages letter by letter.

Since ouija boards are actually on sale in some toy shops these days, a word of advice may be timely here. You've probably already had warnings about 'dabbling in ouija,' generally from experts who've avoided dabbling themselves. These warnings may have left you with the suspicion that there may be dangers associated with the glass – and, indeed, with automatic writing or the use of a planchette. If so, you're absolutely right.

I've yet to come across hard evidence for the major horror stories circulating around the use of ouija – the appearance of demons, heavy poltergeist activity, possession and the rest. But I have seen people get in trouble and while it's easy enough to avoid, you do need to know what sort of genuine problems are likely to arise.

One of the earliest examples I came across involved a group of teenagers who used the ouija very successfully to contact an entity who claimed the boyfriend of one of the sitters was cheating on her with her best friend. The girl was shattered by the news and burst into tears, but it later transpired that the message she'd received was nonsense – her boyfriend was actually as faithful as a Cocker Spaniel.

This telling little incident underlines a basic fact about all forms of 'spirit communication' – the messages you receive may not be true. It's also as well to be aware that the entities may not be who they claim to be. (You should be particularly suspicious of grandiose claims – communicators who introduce themselves as Jesus Christ or Satan, for example.) And you should know some messages aren't even from spirits, but actually originate in your subconscious mind.

Once you get those facts firmly into your head, you'll be guarded against the worst dangers of ouija, planchette or automatic writing. Because the worst dangers almost all arise from taking messages at face value without the application of common sense. That's the attitude which sends idiots up mountains to await the end of the world as predicted by their latest spirit contact.

My own experience has been that useful information *can* come through purported spirit contacts. But to this day I subject every message, without exception, to the following checklist:

- Is this message something you really desperately want to hear, like a prediction you're about to win the Lottery? If so, chances are it comes from your subconscious.

- Is the communicating entity new to you? Newcomers have to go through a long and rigorous process of testing before you should even start to take them seriously.

- Does the communicating entity claim to be a well-known historical personality? If so, be especially suspicious of anything that's said.

Is the message capable of being checked out? If it is, check it. If not, relegate it to your 'Well, maybe, but let's not get too excited file'.

Does the message make sense? A surprising number don't and an equally surprising number of people waste time pretending they do. If a spirit tells you to work towards opening the Watchtower of the Eighteenth Universe through application of the value Pi, you can safely forget it.

Really, truthfully, how likely is the information contained in the message? When I was even younger than I am today and wholly inexperienced in this sort of thing, I was dragged out to a remote island by a group of friends who believed (because a spirit had told them) that it was to be the landing site for seven Exalted Spiritual Masters en route to Sirius in their Flying Saucers. I had an uncomfortable night in miserable weather and the Saucers never turned up. Are you astonished?

Is the information in the message even possible? A small group I know started getting messages from a frenzied spook who claimed to have stolen the body of a NASA astronaut and used it to build a log cabin on Jupiter.

You're welcome to photocopy that checklist and keep it with you.

Hunting For Fairies

The idea that some ghosts might be associated with natural phenomena – and possibly with electrical fields – has led at least a few psychical researchers to wonder if other sightings of supposedly supernatural beings might fall into the same category. Certainly there have been worldwide reports of a whole host of strange visitors ranging from elves and fairies through to gnomes, pixies and sprites of every description.

It's fashionable today to see these beings as belonging to the world of myth – fictional stories with which our ancestors entertained themselves during the long dark evenings. But are we wise to accept this fashionable explanation as the only one possible? The distinguished Irish artist Jim Fitzpatrick once remarked that while it was very easy to dismiss stories of the 'little people' as you sat in the comfort of a city flat, it was a very different matter in the heart of the countryside where everybody around you accepted such creatures as a reality.

Today, of course, even country people increasingly doubt the old stories, yet the reports themselves continue. Only a few years ago, for example, I went to visit friends of mine, a Dutch couple who had only recently returned from a holiday in Sweden. While they were chatting about their experiences, the wife happened to mention a highlight of her trip had been her sighting of a family of trolls.

There was a moment's stunned silence before her husband started to laugh. The woman looked at him blankly. "Trolls don't exist," her husband said at last.

"Yes they do," the wife said confidently. "They're a race of Scandinavian pygmies. Everybody knows that."

She was absolutely convinced this was the truth of the matter – so much so her husband had to show her an encyclopedia entry that defined trolls as mythical. But while she reconsidered her ideas about the nature of trolls, she wouldn't back down about what she'd seen. While driving through a remote area of the Swedish countryside, she'd spotted a troll family by the roadside. The children were little more than 45 cm tall, the adults not much bigger. In appearance they matched the descriptions of trolls that have been a part of Scandinavian mythology for centuries.

Even more peculiar was the case of an American tourist who rented herself a holiday home in a remote area of the west of Ireland. While taking a bath, she suddenly discovered she was being watched by a leprechaun.

Since it was a male leprechaun, modesty overcame any instinct towards psychical research and she shouted at the creature to go away. Since she was, apparently, quite an attractive American tourist, the leprechaun declined to do so. The outcome of the encounter was that they became friends and the woman subsequently met several of the leprechaun's relatives. She eventually published a book describing her experiences in detail and showing photographs of the location where the leprechauns appeared.

Although the best efforts of Hollywood have made leprechauns figures of fun, even in Ireland, reports of sightings continue to emerge, despite the ridicule they attract. While I was living on a country estate in County Kildare, for example, my landlord – a man wholly sceptical about the paranormal – burst white-faced into my home seeking reassurance that he wasn't going mad. The problem, it transpired, was that he'd just seen a leprechaun.

He'd been walking his dogs, two lively terriers, through a little wood on the estate when a peculiar sound made him turn. Behind him, seated on a tree stump, was a tiny, wizened man dressed in brown britches and jerkin with a cloth cap on his head. The creature was so small my landlord realised at once it could not be human. He became extremely excited and said something at the little man in Irish.

The creature simply looked at him, but the dogs, who had been off hunting rabbits, heard the commotion and started to run back, barking furiously. Afraid they might attack his leprechaun, my landlord turned and shouted at them to keep away. When he turned back, the little man had disappeared.

Was my landlord going mad? He was sane enough in all his other activities – he certainly never forgot to collect the rent. Was he simply making up the story as a joke? Perhaps, but he never admitted the prank and at the time he told me, he was obviously a frightened man, trembling with excitement and pale as death. Besides, the area where he'd been walking the dogs had generated other reports of curious appearances.

Mrs Hilda Morgan, the widow of a well-known Welsh novelist, was a guest on the estate. While walking through the same little wood, she happened on the ruin of a 12th century church. Beside the church was the remains of a bathing pool once used by medieval monks from a nearby monastic establishment.

Today, the pool is nothing more than a stone-lined depression discoloured by the barest trickle from a passing stream. But as Mrs Morgan walked into the clearing, she saw at once that the pool was full. Seated on the edge, dangling one foot in the water, was a wood nymph.

Mrs Morgan watched the creature for a few moments then walked back down to the main house to have afternoon tea.

Although confirmed by respectable and apparently reliable witnesses, experiences of this type are so unbelievable that they are difficult to take seriously … unless, of course, you happen to have one yourself.

This is what happened to me in relation to fairies – yes, fairies: the little winged creatures you stopped believing in when you were about five. I'd stopped believing in them too until a few years ago when I was walking through an extraordinarily attractive garden one hot and sunny summer's day.

The garden had an unusually high percentage of belled flowers, notably foxgloves – beautiful but poisonous plants from which the drug digitalis is extracted to treat certain heart conditions. I was admiring a clump when I noticed a small movement out of the corner of my eye. I glanced across without moving my head, expecting to see an insect, perhaps a dragonfly or butterfly.

Instead I saw something that wasn't really there at all: a sort of shimmering in the air. I stood quite still and watched it. The shimmer didn't stay in one place, but flitted at intervals from flower to flower, rather like a bee drinking nectar.

I should tell you I wasn't thinking about fairies at the time. I didn't even imagine the shimmering was in any way paranormal. What I thought – if I thought about it at all really – was that the shimmering was some sort of natural phenomenon, rather like heat haze above a roadway. In fact the shimmering was so like this sort of haze that I wondered if perhaps some flowers generated substantial amounts of heat. It wasn't something I'd ever heard of, but then I'm no expert in gardening.

But I quickly noticed something very odd. The shimmering had a shape. It looked like a silhouette of a small winged figure approximately 7 centimetres tall. What's more, it held the shape as it moved. I leaned forward to look more closely and the 'figure' promptly disappeared.

The whole thing was quite subtle so that I began to wonder if I'd really seen anything at all. But I was intrigued by the fact that the shimmering had a shape – and exactly the same shape flower fairies were supposed to have. Was it possible that flowers generated some sort of local energy field and the shape had convinced people who saw it that they were looking at a little winged figure?

Or could it even be that the shimmering was something far more exciting – the faint, flickering appearance of an otherwise invisible fairy?

I don't know which of these ideas is true, or whether there is a completely different explanation. But I do know what I saw was something other than imagination, not simply because I have seen these little 'energy figures' quite frequently since then, but also because I've been able to teach others to see them too.

If you'd like to take time out from hunting ghosts to go on a fairy hunt, here's how you do it. First, plan to start your investigations in late spring or summer. I've yet to meet anybody able to see energy fairies during winter – I certainly can't – and they become increasingly rare as summer turns to autumn.

Next, find yourself a good-sized clump of belled flowers –

foxgloves, bluebells, fuchsia and the like. They don't have to be in a cultivated garden: I've had many interesting sightings in hedgerows. (You'll find it's quite possible to see the shapes on other flowers as well and even around certain bushes – they like roses, for example – but the highest concentration and the most visible shimmering all seem to be associated with belled flowers.)

Approach your chosen flowers *slowly*. I can't stress this enough. If you go charging over with your hobnails clomping, your chances of seeing anything will be severely reduced. Energy fairies are disturbed by sudden movement. For the same reason, it's a very good idea not to bring your dog or other lively pet along. And if you hunt with friends, make sure they know the rules. While still a metre or so away, stop and watch.

What you should be looking at isn't the flowers themselves. Focus your attention just above a flower. Move your head as little as possible and be on the alert for anything that appears in your peripheral vision (out of the corner of your eye). Be patient. Spotting these little things isn't easy, otherwise everybody would be talking about them.

Allow lots of time and don't give up if you fail to see anything first time out. Remember, most people are capable of spotting the little creatures (assuming they really are creatures) so it's worth a prolonged effort.

Once you've spotted an energy fairy or two, you might like to try your hand at photographing one. I haven't managed it myself yet, but I'd be interested to hear from you if you succeed.

Electronic Ghosts... And How To Catch Them

When I first took an interest in psychical research, there were only five types of ghost a ghosthunter could hunt. These were the five we've examined so far in this handbook – 'grey lady' natural recordings, poltergeists, time slips, spirits of the dead and phantoms of the living.

But that's changed now. There are two new classes of ghost to chase now. The first originally turned up in the sandstone cellar of a 14th century house in Coventry, England. Although once part of a Benedictine Priory, the house is now a Tourist Information Centre and the cellar is open to the public. Some years ago, a haunting started.

A Canadian journalist had the sensation of a balloon being pushed between his shoulder blades. He turned to see the face of a woman peering over his shoulder. A Latvian visitor felt a ghostly presence and an intense chill. An American found her way barred by an invisible entity, as did one of the tour guides.

These and many other reports added up to a very typical haunting, but no ghost was actually involved. Subsequent investigation showed the trouble was associated with a standing wave of 19Hz infrasound. The source of the sound remains a mystery, but similar reports of a haunted workshop were traced to an infrasound wave generated by a fan in a laboratory cupboard.

The association of infrasound with weird phenomena remains to be properly investigated, but the second new category of ghost has now been attracting worldwide attention for some years. This category is known as EVP, or Electronic Voice Phenomenon, and the breakthrough came in 1959 when the Swedish movie producer Friedrich Jürgenson went into the woods near his home to record some birdsong. He was a keen twitcher and had made many recordings before, but this one proved to be different. When he played back the tape, there was a faint voice in the background calling his name.

Jürgenson had heard no voice in the woods, but when he rewound and replayed, there was definitely a voice on the tape. He adjusted the volume and played it again…and again… and again. It was a woman's voice and one he recognised. He grew more and more convinced he was listening to his mother.

The only problem was that his mother had been dead for several years.

This was the first ghost Jürgenson ever recorded, but it proved

not to be the last. More and more voices appeared on his tapes until he had enough material to publish a book about them.

Jürgenson's book, *Rösterna från Rymden* (*Voices from Space*), appeared in Sweden in 1964. In it, he claimed to have recorded the spirit voices of Adolf Hitler and several other well known, but very dead, individuals. Among those who read the book was the Latvian linguist, psychiatrist and psychical researcher, Dr Konstantin Raudive.

Dr Raudive was so intrigued that he contacted Jürgenson to ask if he'd be prepared to demonstrate how he made the recordings. Jürgenson agreed and in April, 1965, they met. Raudive was accompanied by his colleague, Dr Zenta Maurina.

At first the visitors had trouble making out what the voices were saying. They spoke quickly, in fragmented sentences with a peculiar rhythm. But as the tapes were replayed again and again, their ears gradually attuned until they could hear clearly these messages from the dead.

Or at least that's what Jürgenson claimed them to be. Drs Raudive and Maurina had no way of deciding whether he was telling the truth. For all they knew, he might have hired actors to make the tapes and faked the whole thing – the man was, after all, a movie producer.

But when they expressed their doubts, Jürgenson immediately offered to make a brand-new recording there and then. This he did and Raudive listened in astonishment as voices appeared that clearly were not, and could not, be anyone in the room. One of them even answered a chance remark by Dr Maurina. (She said she thought people seemed to be happy and carefree in the Afterlife. The voice said, 'Nonsense!')

This convinced Raudive that Jürgenson wasn't faking the tapes, but not that the voices were spirits of the dead. He decided he needed to make his own recordings. At 9.30 pm on June 10, 1965, he managed the first of many. A taped voice called 'Friedrich, Friedrich.' Then a woman's voice said softly, *'Heute pa nakti. Kennt ihr Margaret, Kon-stantin?'* After a brief pause, the same voice sang, *'Vi tálu! Runá!'* Finally a different female voice said, *'Va a dormir, Margarete!'* The words are a mixture of German, Latvian, English and French. They translate as: 'Frederick, Frederick! Tonight. Do you know Margaret, Konstantin? We are far away! Speak! Go to sleep, Margaret.' Raudive was convinced the message referred to a friend named Margaret who had recently died.

Throughout the remainder of his life, Dr Raudive accumulated more than 30,000 of these mysterious recordings. They included the voices of dead relatives and what seemed to be the voices of several famous people like Tolstoi, who wrote *War and Peace*, the psychiatrist Carl Jung, Russian Premier Josef Stalin, Hitler, the Italian dictator Benito Mussolini and even Britain's wartime leader, Winston Churchill.

In 1968, Dr Raudive published a book in German on his work. Three years later it was translated into English under the title *Breakthrough*. It brought a lot of publicity for the mystery voices and as a result, the tapes underwent substantial scientific tests. These showed a) that there was definitely *something* on the tape, recorded in the same frequency range as human speech and b) it didn't come about through freak intrusions like radio broadcasts, high frequency transmissions or (as one suggestion had it) secret messages from the CIA.

Unlike a lot of work in the ghosthunting field, it turned out that anybody with the right equipment and a little patience could record a 'Raudive voice.' As a result, several hundred thousand have now been put on tape worldwide. Most of them are simple fragments of speech, but since Dr Raudive's death in 1974, several electronics engineers have invested time and energy into devices designed to provide easy, audible, two-way communication with the dead.

One of them, a German named Hans Otto König, demonstrated his live on Radio Luxembourg in 1983. The device was checked for fraud by station technicians and the experiment was carried out by staff members, not König himself. It began on air with one of the station staff asking aloud for a voice to come through. A few seconds later, a voice did. 'Otto König makes wireless with the dead,' it said. The conversation that ensued was interrupted by an assurance from presenter Rainer Holbe that 'on the life of my children' nothing had been manipulated and no one was playing any tricks.

The experiment was just one example of what's now being called 'instrumental transcommunication' – spirit contacts using phones, fax, television and computers. In 1985, an engineer named Klaus Schreiber hit on a method that produced television pictures of the dead. From time to time the images were identified as specific people by electronic voices.

Around the same time, Britain's Kenneth Webster claimed 250 computer-based communications from a 16th century spirit, many of them accompanied by poltergeist phenomena. The text-based communications were consistent with the speech patterns of the time and contained historical details that were later verified.

Two years later, the husband and wife research team of Jules and Maggie Harsh-Fischbach from Luxembourg received a three-page fax from the French science fiction writer Jules Verne (who died in 1905) giving details of the afterlife.

All this would sound utterly unbelievable if it wasn't for the fact that you can record spirit voices for yourself. Dr Raudive used five different methods and four of them require no special equipment, except for one inexpensive item that should be available from a radio hobby shop. To go electronic ghosthunting, you can take your pick from the following:

1 Open Microphone Recording

All you need is an ordinary tape recorder and microphone. Most tape machines have a microphone built in.
Set up your equipment in a quiet room and switch on. Record a little introduction giving your name, the date and the time. Now leave the recorder running in silence for ten or 15 minutes. And that's it! The hard part actually comes after you switch off. You need to rewind the tape and listen for any mystery voice you may have picked up. To do this properly can take you hours. The voices are often brief, fast and very soft spoken so you can miss them altogether on the first few replays of the tape. Even when you catch one, several more replays may be needed to make out the words. You need to take time to train your ears.

2 Radio Recording

For this you need a tape recorder and a radio. You can record with an open microphone, but it's better to attach the radio to your recorder with a direct jack-plug. Or you may be lucky enough to get hold of a combined radio/cassette recorder. Since these allow you to record radio programmes, they're ideal for EVP.

Begin by tuning the radio to an inter-frequency – a place on the tuning scale where no station is broadcasting and the radio just produces the sort of hiss technicians call white noise. Now start recording and again let the tape run for 15 minutes or so.

As with open mike recordings, you'll have to train your ears to pick up the voices during playback.

3 Combined Radio Jack and Microphone Recording

This involves connecting a recorder to a radio via a jack, while at the same time recording the radio broadcast through a microphone attached to the same recorder. The session proceeds exactly as before, using a white noise inter-frequency. For some reason the method produces voices that are a little clearer.

4 Diode Recording

This is the only method that needs special equipment, specifically a diode. A diode is a small item that functions as a very primitive radio receiver. It can't be tuned or anything fancy like that, but it does produce very good quality spirit voices. All you need do is attach it to a short (6-8 cm) aerial, then plug it into your recorder via a jack. Set recording sensitivity to its highest level and feel free to experiment with the length of the aerial.

Once you've cut your teeth on a few recorded spirit voices, you might like to take a crack at the big one – a spirit face on your television set. The experiment requires a video camera and while these are still hideously expensive, more and more homes have them so there's a reasonable chance you may be able to borrow one.

The technique used is actually very simple. You connect your video camera to the TV set and point the camera at the screen. With both switched on, you turn the television to a dead channel so only static appears on the screen. The video camera records the static and feeds it back into the TV for display. This produces a swirling electronic fog. Leave the camera running and, with luck, you should see images gradually emerge

Glossary

Automatic Writing Messages produced by allowing a spirit to take control of your hand and write with it.

Clairvoyance The ability to see or sense objects or events at a distance without mechanical aids.

Diode A small piece of electrical equipment used together with a radio to record voices of the dead. A diode is actually a semiconductor allowing the flow of current in one direction only and having two terminals, but you don't really need to know that.

Dowsing A method of finding underground water and other things (including ghosts) using a special set of rods or a forked stick.

Ectoplasm A cloud-like white substance, apparently produced from the body of a medium, that spirits can mould to give themselves visible appearance.

Electronic Voice Phenomenon Mysterious messages recorded on tape that are believed to be voices of the dead.

ESP Extra-Sensory Perception, a blanket term for paranormal abilities like telepathy, clairvoyance and precognition.

EVP Electronic Voice Phenomenon.

Exorcism A religious ceremony designed to get rid of ghosts, demons and similar entities.

Flying Pencil Ancient Chinese name for automatic writing.

Grey Lady A phantom of either sex that repeats the same actions over and over. Many psychical researchers believe this type of ghost is not a spirit at all, but rather some sort of natural recording.

Hypnosis An induced state in which the subject is compelled to accept any suggestion given by the hypnotist.

Levitation The ability to rise and float in the air without any form of support.

Medium Somebody who claims to be in contact with the spirits of the dead.

OOBE Out-of-Body Experience.

Ouija A device designed to allow people to receive messages from the dead spelled out letter by letter.

Out-of-Body Experience The sensation of leaving your body and moving around like a ghost.

Parapsychology The scientific study of weird phenomena, especially where it involves the human mind.

Pepper's Ghost A technical illusion that creates an apparent ghost on the stage of a theatre.

Planchette A device designed to allow people to receive written messages from spirits.

Poltergeist A noisy or mischievous ghost, that sometimes causes damage.

Precognition The ability to see or sense an event before it actually happens.

Psychical Research The scientific investigation of ghosts and other strange phenomena. For more information, contact the Society for Psychical Research at 49, Marloes Road, Kensington, London W8 6LA or log on to *www.spr.ac.uk*.

Psychokinesis The ability to move solid objects using only the power of your mind.

Séance A gathering of people – usually Spiritualists – attempting to make contact with the dead.

Sitter Someone attending a séance or consulting a medium.

Spiritualist Someone who believes spirits of the dead can contact the living, especially through a medium. There are several Spiritualist churches where this belief is incorporated into a religion.

Telepathy Direct mind-to-mind contact.

Trance A semi-conscious state in which people show little or no response to anything going on around them.

Ghosthunter Report Form

Date .... Time ....

Place ....

Location Description

....

....

....

....

Ghost type

....

Sighting conditions

Visibility ....

Lighting ....

Weather ....

Witnessed by:

Name ....

Address ....

....

....

Name ....

Address ....

....

....

Name ....

Address ....

....

....

Name ....

Address ....

....

....

Appearance

Shape ....

Size ....

Colour ....

Brightness ....

Transparency ....

Ease of visibility ....

Sketch ghost here:

Behaviour

Movement ....

Sound ....

Speech ....

Other Communication (if any) ....

....

....

....

....

....

General

Prior reports on this site? Yes ☐ No ☐

Were you looking for a ghost? Yes ☐ No ☐

Any physical contact? Yes ☐ No ☐

Associated Phenomena

....

....

....

....

....

....

How long did the experience last?

....

Additional Comments

....

....

....

....

....

....

Afterword

If you've got this far, you're now well equipped to embark on one of the most interesting – and important – areas of investigation open to you.

There's no doubt at all that ghosts and other strange phenomena actually exist. Even the most hardened sceptics only argue about whether they're actually supernatural.

Nor is there any doubt that even the most experienced of experts are still at a loss for definite explanations.

Which means there's lots of room for you to make your name. Because you could be the one who finally proves what ghosts and strange phenomena are all about.

Good hunting.

Herbie Brennan, Carlow, Ireland, 2003

Index